FREEING JASPER

THE 707 SERIES
BOOK 2

RILEY EDWARDS

Freeing Jasper
The 707 Freedom Series

This book is dedicated to all the brave men and women who serve or have served in the United States Armed Forces. There are no words to properly convey the sacrifices they make and the appreciation I have for the cost of their service.

A special thanks to the sailors aboard the USS Nimitz (CVN68). I wrote this book while thinking about her crew, especially my daughter who is currently aboard in support of Operation Inherent Resolve. Godspeed sailors. BRAVO ZULU!

To the men in the 3rd ID (Infantry Division) Rock of Marne - Fort Stewart, Georgia: As the 3rd Combat Aviation Brigade and 3rd Sustainment Brigade, 3rd Infantry Division begin their deployment in support of Operation Resolute Support may God be with you.

– Dogface soldiers, CAN DO!

The world lost 31 Heroes 06 Aug 2011. SOC SEAL John W. Faas was among the crew that died that day. Even in death, John continues to inspire all those who knew him and love him. He is not forgotten - never forgotten. His sacrifice and that of his family's reminds us that freedom is never free.

We sleep soundly in our beds because rough men stand ready in the night to visit violence on those who would do us harm.

Whether it was the writer George Orwell, the essayist Richard Grenier, or the Washington Times columnist Rudyard Kipling who originally wrote those words matters not. The sentiment rings true. We are only afforded the luxuries we have because rough men are willing to stand at the ready. Chief Faas was one of those men.

31 heroes – From a grateful nation.

PROLOGUE

Jasper

"Yo! Anyone home?" I walked in the front door without knocking.

"You know Lenox is gonna give you shit for just walking in his house," Levi said laughing as I opened the door and let myself in.

"That's what makes it so fun." What could I say? Riling Lenox up was amusing.

"I'm in the kitchen," Lily yelled.

Levi and I made our way to the kitchen, and my stomach growled. Lily had a metric shit ton of food spread out over the counter. God, I loved that woman. Maybe I'd consider not annoying Lenox today, in appreciation for him bringing us Lily.

"Hey, Lily," Levi said and pulled her in for a hug.

"Thanks for having us over, everything looks great," I noted.

After Lily came to Georgia and moved in with Lenox, and especially after Carter was born, the team had taken to backyard barbeques and poker at their house. It was a far cry from our nights together bar hopping after we got home from a mission. I was happy for Lenox, him and Lily both. After all their years apart, they deserved to be happy.

"One of these days I'm gonna beat your ass for walking into my house without knocking. And keep your voices down, I just put Carter to sleep," Lenox commented when he came in the room.

"Doubtful," I shot back.

"Doubtful I'll do it? Or doubtful I can? Because I think I proved not too long ago I can put you on your ass."

He wished.

"Man, you sucker punched me. It doesn't count," I said, picking up a cracker and shoving it in my mouth.

"You're so full of shit. I warned you I was gonna kick your ass. It wasn't my fault you didn't believe me."

He did. He warned me the night I told him that Lily was pregnant and I had kept it from him. I didn't regret keeping Lily's secret, I would do it again. They needed time to get their shit together and heal from everything that had happened. They had both said things to each other they didn't mean. I knew a little bit about saying things that you could never take back – I didn't want my friend to suffer the same fate I had.

In an effort to push Lily away, in some misguided effort to protect her, Lenox had said some pretty brutal stuff to her. Including lying to her, telling her he had never loved her. When the truth was, he had loved her his whole life. It was all for naught when Lily was kidnapped and held in the Bahamas by a madman. After we rescued Lily, she knew she was pregnant, but hadn't told anyone. I made the decision to not tell Lenox. Lily had already made up her mind she was going to run. There was nothing that Lenox could've said to make her stay. It would've only further driven a wedge between them. I let Lily leave without telling Lenox. They both needed time. When her time ran out, the team and I took Lenox to her. In the end, it was the right choice. Lenox and Lily were happily married with a son they both adored.

Only, Lenox didn't actually give me a beat down or kick my ass, he sucker punched me in the face, and I didn't hit him back. That's how men worked their shit out. It was easy; a man gets pissed, he punches another man in the face, we move on. It was so much easier than what women did – bitch and drag it on, forever rehashing it every chance they got.

"No more talking about the fight. We're here to eat, drink, and play poker," Lily chastised.

"But Lily, this is what real men do. We talk about fighting, fucking, and killing bad guys," Levi helpfully explained.

The look of shock on Lily's face was hysterical. I knew she thought that Levi was the most mild-mannered out of the group because he rarely cursed in front of her. Boy was she wrong. We all had our own special skillset when we were in the field. Each of us brought something unique that made our team the best there was. Levi was ice-cold when we were on a mission. Not even I could turn off my emotions the way he could, and he was brutal when he needed to be. And the cursing? He had Lily snowed; that man came up with some pretty creative words for tangos.

"Seriously?" Lily asked.

I had to laugh when Lily turned to Lenox for help.

"Well, sweetheart, he's not wrong," Lenox confirmed.

I thought I heard Lily mumble *men* under her breath, but there was a knock at the door before I could comment.

"For tonight, while I have a friend over, can we please limit the talk about fighting, fucking, and killing?"

"We'll see what we can do," Shane replied, smiling at his wife.

"Is she hot?" I couldn't help asking. I didn't bother hiding my enjoyment of women around my team. I know they probably thought I got laid more than I actually did, I just didn't bother correcting them.

"Not answering that," Lily shouted back as she went for the door.

"Dude, what happened to the blonde from last night?" Levi asked.

Yes, the blonde. She was sexy as hell and fake. Every part of her from her glued-on lashes to the porno-style moans. Boring. A dime a dozen. We both had fun and parted ways. No hard feelings.

"Do you want details or the cliff notes?" I joked.

"Not even worth the normal week?" Lenox laughed.

"She kicked me outta her bed with a thanks-for-coming-don't-call-again. I smiled and left," I explained.

Levi or Lenox said something, but I'd lost interest when I heard the sweetest voice come from the other room. I couldn't make out the words, something about whiskey maybe. It was the tone of her voice, the cadence. The kind of voice that would soothe and lull you to sleep. Just the sound of it alone hit me in the gut. She wouldn't fake her moans, she would enjoy her man, actually *feel* him.

"Come in. The guys are in the kitchen, and if you want to eat, we'd better hurry," I heard Lily say.

Holy fuck.

In walked the prettiest woman I had ever seen. Long midnight hair that was made to have a man wrap around his hand. Crystal blue eyes made even more beautiful by her skin tone, not makeup. I didn't even think the girl was wearing any. Her beauty was all her – all real, no pretense, nothing fake.

"Hi, Emily. Nice to see you again, thanks for coming over," Lenox said.

His voice pulled me from my stupor, reminding me I was in front of my team.

"Hey, Lenox. Thanks for having me," the woman, Emily, replied.

"This is Jasper and Levi, Shane's teammates." Lily pointed at each of us.

"Hi. I'm Emily." Her sweet voice was even better close up.

"Nice to meet you," Levi politely said.

"Yo," I greeted. When her eyes came to me, I could've sworn I saw a flash of interest. I had to know for sure so I added a wink.

Emily blushed. Hell yeah!

"You from around here, Emily?" I asked for no other reason than I wanted to hear her voice.

Before Emily could answer, there was a honk from out front that drew everyone's attention away.

"That must be Clark," Lenox said.

Shit, I forgot. Another reason we were here today. We were going to build Carter a swing set. I followed Lenox and Levi to the front door without getting to hear Emily's answer.

The door shut behind us and Lenox turned to me. "Lily will have your balls if you fuck with Emily, brother. And while I'm not fond of that visual, better she removes yours than mine."

"Fuck with her? I don't want to fuck with her," I told him.

"You didn't exactly hide the fact you were eye fucking her," Levi added.

"I was not eye fucking her. If I was, she would've been panting. I won't lie, she's fucking gorgeous."

"But? There's normally a *but* after the phrase, *I won't lie*," Levi asked.

"No buts. Just acknowledging the fact, she's beautiful."

Lenox stared at me, something weird working behind his eyes. "What?" I prompted.

"Huh. I'm not used to you calling women beautiful or gorgeous. Sexy and hot are your normal adjectives."

"You're way overthinking this. Let's get this lumber in the backyard so we can eat," I said.

Damn, nothing gets past that fucker. The truth was she was both hot and sexy, but it seemed beneath her to describe her that way. She wasn't some barfly I wanted to take home for the night. Not that I wouldn't mind some alone time with her. But more than that, I wanted to talk to her, take her to dinner so I could hear her laugh. I bet she had a great laugh.

EMILY

"What's that look for?" I asked Lily after the guys left the room.

"No look," she answered and busied herself straightening up the food trying to hide her discomfort.

"Liar. You think I'd fall for a lame pick-up attempt? I'm not stupid enough to fall for a man like Jasper. Besides, I haven't been with a man since Steven. I think if I am going to start dating again I need to start with training wheels. And that man looks like he's as high speed as they come." I tried to put her at ease. Most of what I'd said was true. The other parts? I was saying them more to myself than her.

"I don't think you're stupid. And I love Jasper like a brother. I don't have a bad word to say about him. But he..." she trailed off.

"He's a dog." I laughed. "A man that sexy can be. I'm sure he has women throwing themselves at him."

I was sure not many women would be able to resist Jasper if he turned all of his attention on them. His messy brown hair was cut short on the sides in standard military regulations. It made him look sexy in a *I don't give a shit* way. And his deep blue eyes told a story if you really looked before he turned on the charm.

"What the hell?" Lily said, looking over my shoulder into the backyard.

I turned around to look and holy dear God the sight was amazing. The guys were carrying lumber, muscles bulged and flexed under their T-shirts. Even from a distance, I could see Jasper's shirt pulling tight over his impressive biceps.

"I don't know what the hell they're doing, but I admit I am enjoying the view," I said.

Lily opened the sliding glass door and hollered, "What are you doing?"

"Building a swing set," a man answered.

"A swing set?" she returned.

My attention was pulled from Lily's conversation, and I was fully engrossed in watching Jasper move. Just his walk exuded power.

"You know, for junior," Levi added.

"You do know that the baby won't be able to play on the swing set for years, right?" Lily told them.

"So?" Jasper spoke up. "No time like the present."

"You're crazy. All of you have lost your minds. I don't know what to say."

"Don't say anything, Lily. We want to make sure that Carter's taken care of while we can," the man who I had not met yet answered.

Lily's face softened, and her tone changed. "Thank you," she called back.

"No problem," he answered.

She shut the door when the guys disappeared around the corner of the house and turned to me.

"That's sweet they're doing all this," I said.

"I'm sorry. I'm new to all of this and forget sometimes," she apologized.

Ah, I understood what she was apologizing for. "Don't be silly. There's nothing to be sorry for. They are going a little overboard out there, but I do understand. We never know how much time we have with them. One of the perils of falling in love with a man like that." I stopped and sucked in a deep breath. I understood all too well. The love I had for Steven was far different than the love that Lily and her husband had. But I knew the loss nonetheless. "Hold on tight, Lily, and enjoy every minute. Soak it all up. You'll need it to get you through deployments and training assignments. And God forbid if the unthinkable happens, you'll need all the goodness and love he gave you to get through that, too."

"Did you soak up enough?" she asked.

"I thought I did, but now I'm not so sure. My tank's running low," I answered.

I hated not being able to tell Lily the truth. I wasn't keeping the truth from her because I didn't trust her. I was protecting Steven's reputation. He deserved my loyalty, even in death.

"Does it bother you being over here, around us?"

"Hell-to-the-no, sister. I love you and Lenox. Just because Steven is gone, doesn't mean I want to lose my family. Right after it happened, I was afraid I would lose that, too. The Army is my life, and I still love it."

"Good. Because I love you woman."

That felt good. I didn't have a lot of friends. My life was wrapped up in being a single mom. Jason was all that I had left.

"Now, let's grab a drink and sit on the deck. I wanna watch the guys carry the lumber." She laughed. Lily grabbed the baby monitor while I grabbed a beer and we made our way to the back deck.

It didn't take all but ten minutes before the guys

were all shirtless as they continued to make trips back and forth to the front of the house.

"Holy shit," I mumbled.

"You got that right," she said. I laughed, and she cocked her eyebrow. "I might be married, but I'm not dead. The first time Adam and Anthony met the guys, Anthony called them the badass brigade. I think he should've called them the sexy brigade."

Lily had mentioned her friends Adam and Anthony before. She'd met them while living in South Carolina – they were house flippers. She had shown me some of the designs she had worked up for them. She was excellent.

"There's nothing like a well-trained, well-toned military man. I have to admit, as much as I swore I would never be with a soldier again, I think I'm ruined. I don't know how I could ever date a civilian."

"You're such a snob." Lily giggled.

"That's better than being called a depend-a-pota-mous. Which is what I'd be called if I ever dated another soldier again."

"Who cares what anyone else thinks. Fuck 'em."

"Dating is so far off my radar it doesn't even matter. But I can sit back and enjoy all the yummy sexy goodness walking around your yard, that's for damn sure."

It had been a long time since I'd been with a man. Damn near rounding on six years. My friend Connor had been trying to get me to date again, but I didn't know if that was a good idea. Unless Jasper asked me on a date. A girl could dream. Jasper did not look like the type of man that dated women, he looked more like a super-yummy one-night stand. Which I wouldn't be opposed to either.

The guys finished unloading the wood and sat on the deck with us. The new guy Clark was kind of quiet and watchful. When the rest joked and laughed, he joined in but in a more somber type of way. Jasper was an insatiable flirt. He did it in a way that was fun rather than lewd. The more relaxed he became around me, the less he guarded his stare. There was definitely something behind his playful banter, something painful he covered up with jokes. I actually felt kind of bad thinking that he was a dog. I bet that the women he was with didn't even bother to see him. All they saw were the sexy eyes and a lazy smile.

Jasper

After we'd finished eating on the deck, we moved to the living room to play poker. I couldn't remember the last time I laughed so hard with a woman that wasn't Lily. Emily was a firecracker. She had a comeback for everything I had to say. Through most of dinner her attention was on me. There was something about her that was refreshing. I had been gulping down pond water, and she was the purest of springs. I wanted a sip of her so badly. I was still puzzling out how I was going to ask her to dinner without sounding like a complete dumb-ass. It was getting late, and I was running out of money. Lily and Emily were killing it tonight. They had damn near broke me.

"How's Jason?" Lenox asked Emily after he finished dealing the cards.

Shit, I hadn't thought that she might have a man. I'd never poached another man's woman; however, I would make an exception for Emily.

"He's good. He's at my mom's house for the rest of the week. She's spoiling him rotten and enjoying some time with him before school starts," Emily answered.

What? Her man is spending time with her mom?

"Who's Jason?" I asked.

"My son," Emily answered, and her face lit up.

My vision blurred and the world tilted. Fuck, she had a kid. I took a long swallow of my beer. I felt Lenox's stare burning fire into my chest, but I refused to look at him.

"That's cool," I said praying my voice didn't crack.

Carter's cry cut through the room. It was time for me to go.

CHAPTER ONE

Emily

"Emily?"

"Yes?" I looked up from the coins I was counting and straight into a set of familiar piercing blue eyes. They were almost identical in color to my own.

Jasper.

I hadn't seen him since a barbeque at Lily's house six-months prior. He looked even better than I remembered him, more like a rugged cowboy than the soldier I knew him to be. Jasper worked at the 707 research battalion with Lily's husband, Lenox.

I wasn't sure exactly what they did at the 707, and Lily said very little about where her husband went when he left on assignment. One time she told me the team was out of town auditing another base. My best guess was they inspected equipment records and made sure the supply personnel was keeping an accurate accounting of the gear when it was returned after deployment. He looked damn good for someone who sat behind a desk all day.

"Hey. I didn't know you worked here," Jasper said, trying his best not to show how uncomfortable he was.

The flirty, playful tone he had at the barbeque was painfully absent. The day I met Jasper, he spent the afternoon talking and joking with me. It had been nice to speak to someone who knew nothing about my past and didn't treat me like I was a broken widow. For a few short hours, I felt normal. That was until Lenox asked me about Jason. The mere mention of my son had silenced Jasper. Minutes later, Lily's infant son had woken up and Jasper all but ran out the door making an excuse it was late and not wanting to intrude on family time.

"Yeah, about five years now. We are short a teller today, so I came up front to help out. I'm actually a loan officer," I explained. "Payday. You know how the first and fifteenth are around an Army base. If Uncle Sam doesn't direct deposit, the boys wanna cash their checks." Now I was babbling. God, why was I so awkward?

"Guess that's why I've never seen you."

"I'm actually closing out my drawer. But Beverly can help you." I pointed to the teller station next to mine.

"Yeah, okay. Sorry. It was nice seeing you again." Jasper picked up his deposit slip off the counter and started to move to Beverly's station.

"You, too."

Wow, that was...uncomfortable. I thought back to the day I met Jasper and sighed. When I had walked into Lily's kitchen, I thought I had died and gone to *sexy heaven*. The heaven where only super-hot guys got to go. The first thing I had noticed about Jasper was his smile. It came fast and easy, but if you paid attention, you could see it was put on. There was no doubt he used his good looks to his advantage. He could charm a nun out of her habit with his slick wink and baby blues. Damn, he had gorgeous eyes and dark lashes that were long enough to make any woman jealous.

Lily had tried to warn me off Jasper in her own sweet, nice way. She didn't have it in her to come right out and tell me he was a manwhore, so I let her off the hook and told her I knew he was a dog. It wasn't like I was looking for a man anyway. And if I was, Jasper was so far out of my league it wasn't even funny. I was still playing Tee-ball, and he was in the majors.

I was a single mom with a dead husband and more responsibilities than I cared to think about. He was single, hot, and out for fun. My fun ended six years ago when I got pregnant, and all the responsibility fell squarely on my shoulders eighteen months ago when my husband died.

No, I needed training wheels, not a man like Jasper. But he was oh so nice to look at.

The loud voices and commotion by the bank's front door made me roll my eyes. I hated when the first of the month fell on a Friday. It seemed like every young Army Private came in after they were done with their work day to cash their checks and hit the bars. They were loud and obnoxious and were always in a hurry. Maybe I was being overly dramatic because part of me was jealous of their carefree life. I did not regret having my son so young. Hell in many ways he saved my life. Or at least made me grow up and stop making bad choices. But, I did miss the days when I didn't stress out over everything. I had almost forgotten what it felt like to have fun. Until I spent a few hours in

Jasper's presence and his over-the-top flirting made me smile.

I looked up when two hands smacked the counter in front of me.

"Did you hear me, honey?" a man yelled.

"Huh?"

I turned from the bill counting machine to find a man in a black ski mask leaning over the counter.

Holy fuck!

"I said to keep your hands above the counter and put all your cash into the bag," the man repeated, tossing a duffle in front of me.

"Seriously? How am I supposed to get the cash out of my drawer that's under the counter if you want me to keep my hands above the counter?"

Was he for real? A duffle bag? This idiot had seen too many Hollywood bank heist movies. I wouldn't need to hit the panic button. We were on post. The guard gate would have record and video of everyone who entered the base. Post 9/11, all bases tightened security. He could take all the money and never be able to leave the base with it.

"Listen, bitch, just put the money in the bag. If you think about trying to call for help, everyone in this building dies."

I looked over the man's shoulder and belatedly

noticed two more men, all holding assault rifles and what looked to be standard issue reflex sights on the top rails of their weapons. I wondered if they stole those guns from the Army's armory. Maybe Lenox's team should do an audit of their own base.

The reality of the situation hit, and I froze. The bank was being robbed by three armed masked gunmen, and all I was thinking about was if they stole their guns. What the hell was wrong with me? Screw the money and if they could get off base. I didn't want to die. My son had already lost one parent. With shaky hands, I started to pull the bills off the counting machine, half of them falling on the floor.

"Careful, bitch," the man scolded.

A loud crash at Beverly's station caught my attention. Jasper had jumped over the counter and was now on the employee's side of the partition.

"What the fuck do you think you're doing?" one of the guys holding a rifle yelled and pointed his gun at Jasper.

"Helping you assholes get your money. You've scared the hell out of these ladies."

Thank God there were no customers in the bank. Two other tellers and the branch manager were all the employees left. And Jasper! Jasper was here, too.

Too bad one of the guys from the Ranger battalion wasn't in here cashing his check. Not that I didn't think Jasper could take care of himself in a fight, but Rangers were trained for this type of stuff.

"Em, I want you to stay calm and put the money in the bag." Jasper was standing behind me talking softly into my ear. "When one of them asks to be taken to the vault, I want you to tell both of the other tellers to take him. I want you to stay out front with me."

I shoved the money from the machine into the bag and passed it back to the man standing in front of me. He handed me an empty bag. "Now the money from the drawer," he demanded. "You go back to the vault." He pointed at Beverly.

"You need two tellers to go open the vault. This late in the day it will take two employee codes to unlock," I lied.

Jasper squeezed my calf, scaring the shit out of me. When did he kneel down?

"Both of you go." The man waved to both Beverly and Ashline. "Mr. One, go with them. Mr. Two, how are we on time?" he asked.

"Fine. We still have like six minutes," a man I presumed was Mr. Two answered.

Real original code names. Not!

"Hurry up and get the next drawer. Hey, tough guy, make sure you get all the cash off the floor."

Jasper stood up and put the money he had collected off the floor into the new bag I was holding. The man in front of me walked to Beverly's station and leaned over the counter looking toward the vault.

Jasper took advantage of the masked man being distracted and spoke softly. "When I call out *red*, I want you to drop and lie flat on the ground. Do not move from that position. Copy that?" he instructed.

"Okay," I whispered, my hands still shaking as I stuffed all the bills into the bag. All three open teller drawers had been handed over.

What now?

I didn't understand what Jasper was doing, but if all I had to do was lie on the ground, I was good with it. I wanted to tell him not to do anything crazy, I didn't want to see him hurt over money but he moved away from me too fast. All the fine hairs on the back of my neck started to prickle. I looked around the lobby and Mr. Two, the timekeeper, was staring at me. There was something in the way he looked at me that scared the shit out of me, the fact he had a gun basically pointed at me notwithstanding. His glare was fixated on me. His mask obscured his features, and he was too far away for me to make out the color of his eyes.

"Red," Jasper yelled. I dropped to the ground, and my world exploded in gunfire and the sound of shattering glass.

Gunfire in a small space was not like what you saw on the TV. It was ear-piercingly loud. I couldn't cover my ears enough to drown out the deafening pops. I scooted farther under the counter trying to gain as much protection as I could, and I hoped that Beverly and Ashline were safe. Beverly was a single mom like me; she had a cute three-year-old daughter who needed her. And Chuck, the lazy bank manager, I bet he didn't even know we were being robbed. He spent most of the day locked in his office doing God knows what. It wasn't work, that was for sure.

The gunfire stopped, and I debated whether or not to stay down like Jasper had told me. What if he was injured and needed help? I had no way of knowing if I stayed cowering under my station. I slowly crawled out looking left, then right. I couldn't see anything, and I had to move farther out, and just as I looked left again a pair of black boots stopped right in front of my face. Damn, how did I not hear someone walking up? My eyes traveled up the khaki cargo pants and stopped at the gun pointing at my head. I didn't bother looking up any farther. This was it. I was going to die on my hands and knees on the bank floor leaving my son without a mother. I closed my eyes and prayed my son knew how much I loved him. My mom would make sure Jason was okay.

A gunshot rang out, and I waited for the pain to register. Nothing. There was no pain, only a lingering ringing in my ears. I opened my eyes to find a crumpled body on the ground in front of me, blood pouring out of the black mask. I couldn't move, and no sound left my mouth as relief washed over me. I was alive.

"Em, up you go," Jasper said from beside me. I couldn't pull my gaze from the dead man in front of me. "Close your eyes," he commanded.

I couldn't. I was captivated by the dark red liquid pooling around his head. That could've been me. That would've been, if...

"Emily!" Jasper yelled, finally breaking the spell. I scrambled to stand up, Jasper reaching down to pull me up and into his arms. "I want you to listen to me very carefully. I want you to keep your eyes closed while I get you out of here. You're going to the manager's office until the MPs and local police get here."

"Ashline and Beverly?" I asked.

"They're already in there," he answered.

I was relieved he reached them in time and got them to safety. If I was so relieved then why did I feel a pang of hurt that he had saved the others before me? In reality, I was no one to him. Just because I had thought about him hundreds of times over the last six months didn't mean anything.

"Thank God," I whispered.

Jasper picked me up, and I closed my eyes as he walked us through the bank to the worthless branch manager's office.

"No one questions Emily until I get back. The Commander is on his way down now. I'll be back when I'm done talking to him."

My eyes shot open to see who Jasper was talking to.

"Levi?"

"Hi, darlin', let's get you inside." Levi opened the door allowing Jasper to enter.

Beverly and Ashline were huddled together in the corner crying. There was a suit jacket draped over the top half of a slumped over body at Chuck's desk.

"Is that?" I asked.

"Yes," he answered.

"Is he?" I continued.

"Yes. Sorry, we cannot move him until the police come," Jasper explained.

What the hell was going on?

CHAPTER TWO

Jasper

What a clusterfuck. The Commander was going to flip his shit when he showed up.

"How's Emily?" Lenox asked.

"Uninjured," I answered knowing damn well he was asking about her emotional state not whether or not she'd been hit.

The truth was, I hadn't asked her. I was still trying to get myself under control, and not from the danger of the situation. I'd been in much tighter spots than three amateurs with guns playing at robbing a bank. Hell, I had traveled the world going up against every known terrorist group and many that NATO kept under wraps. The 707 was the government's secret weapon. We were the team that was sent in when there needed to be complete deniability. Our missions were off the books – black ops. On paper, the 707 was a research and development group, paper pushers that audited supply clerks and tested new equipment.

What I wasn't used to was the fear I felt when Emily came out from under the counter before I gave the all clear. My blood ran cold when the douchebag pointed his gun at her head. There was something unexplainably different seeing Emily shaking in fear while a gun was trained on her than when it was one of the guys. Not that they shook in fear, ever. But I had seen each of them in the crosshairs before and never felt the terror that rushed my body when it was her. Maybe it was simply because she was a woman.

"Do you know the amount of paperwork you've created with this little stunt?" the Commander's voice boomed. "You just couldn't let these little fuckbags take the cash and go. No, you had to cause a shit storm that is going to take a hell of a lot of creative bullshitting to get you out of this mess."

I didn't bother answering the Commander, I knew he wasn't done with his dressing down yet.

"And if it wasn't bad enough, you had to call

your team into this cluster. Please tell me you pulled the tapes."

"Affirmative," Lenox answered.

"Why don't you break this down Barney style and walk me through why you thought it was a good idea to kill two bank robbers on American soil. You're not playing in the sandbox, Christ Almighty. At least I can partially contain the intel on this base."

Yep, the Commander was pissed.

"I called in my team for backup, they're easier to contain. And frankly, I don't trust an MP to have my six. I had no intention of killing any of them. My plan was to disarm and detain. The plan was shot to shit when douchebag number one pointed his gun in my goddamn face. I took exception to the threat and feared for my personal safety. After he was properly dealt with, douchebag number two pointed his gun at me, I couldn't get a clean shot off so I only winged him and he fled the scene. Douche number three took one between the eyes when in his infinite wisdom he thought it was a good idea to point a gun at Emily's head."

I hadn't meant to mention Emily by name. Lenox's eyebrows shot to his hairline at the same time the Commander asked, "So, this is personal?"

"Not at all," I answered. Damn, I cannot believe I slipped.

"What then? Not enough action. You thought you'd swoop in and save the day?"

"No, sir. I was just trying to save the Army's investment. It'd be expensive to train another operator with my skill set."

"Wiseass. What did the hostages see?" he asked.

"Not a damn thing. When Levi and I entered from the rear, both women were hugging each other in the corner out of the line of sight. Levi stayed with them, and I entered the lobby to provide backup for Jasper. The situation was contained by the time I entered," Lenox explained.

The Commander's face was bright red, and I actually thought he might stroke out at any moment.

"Contained? You call this contained. What about the other girl?"

"She was under her desk and didn't see anything." I respected the hell out of the Commander. He was a good man and had served on the front lines, but if he thought I was going to stand down while three innocent lives were in danger, he didn't know me very well. "I apologize for your trouble but not for my actions. They were justified, and I'm prepared for whatever action needs to be taken."

"Yeah, yeah, I know, you'll fall on your sword. I need to know Lenox, did you or Levi fire your weapons?"

"No," Lenox assured the Commander.

"And what about you, Andy Griffith? Did you fire your personal weapon?"

Now, who was the wiseass?

"No. You'll find that body number one's cause of death is from a hangman's fracture. I used his gun, thought I'd save my ammo."

The Commander uttered a few more expletives under his breath and walked around the lobby shaking his head as he went. I glanced at Lenox, taken aback by the wide smile plastered on his face.

Before I could ask why the hell he was smiling, the Commander stopped in front of us. "I'll send in a crew to scrub the scene. I want that videotape at the hangar in twenty minutes. I want a sworn statement from all three hostages they didn't see anything. We don't have time for this. I have a lock on Roman's pilot. I want him brought in. If Roman was telling the truth before he was taken out and he had an inside man in our ranks, I want to know before I send another team out."

Now I understood why the Commander was over-the-top mad. It wasn't like I had caused an international incident. Hell, I was within my legal rights to protect myself from personal danger. He didn't want me caught up in an investigation that would make it impossible to leave on a mission. He could, obviously, waiver me through the system, but that would draw attention to me. Attention that we couldn't afford.

The Commander left, leaving me alone with Lenox. "What's the smile for?"

"You snapped his neck? Christ, there's something wrong with you. Why can't you just shoot bad guys like a normal person? It's always up close and personal for you."

I didn't bother answering. I didn't like having to kill anyone, but I would if I had to. Lenox was referencing my ability to eliminate a threat with my bare hands or blade if necessary. Some men preferred the impersonal nature of a gun. We were all trained to kill by any means, but some men faltered when it came to wet work, so to speak. Not me.

I opened the door to the manager's office to find Emily sitting in a chair by herself. Levi was softly speaking to the other two women who were still crying. I was surprised that Emily had remained calm and collected through the whole ordeal. A sense of pride welled in me. A feeling I didn't want to examine.

"Hey." I knelt down in front of her and waited for her to look at me.

"Hi," she spoke so softly I could barely hear her.

"The Commander needs you and the other tellers to sign a statement. Do you think you can do that?" Emily nodded. "And ask the other two tellers, as well?"

"Sure."

Maybe she wasn't handling this as well as I had first thought. She was staring into my eyes, but hers were flat and lifeless. My heart squeezed. I didn't like the fear I saw. Without another word, she got up, forcing me to stand as well. I watched as she walked over to the other two women and spoke to them. Hugging them both trying to soothe them. They nodded at whatever Emily was saying to them. Levi was standing closest to them and handed Emily a yellow legal pad. The first woman jotted something down on the tablet and handed it to the other woman. She did the same thing and gave it to Emily. After Emily wrote her statement, she walked back to me and handed me the pad.

"Here. Is it okay if I leave now?" she asked.

There was no spunk in her tone, no playful smile

on her lips like there was the first time I met Emily. She was a beautiful woman, but what made her absolutely stunning was her sassy sense of humor and smile. She had been easy to talk to that afternoon. Her playfulness was painfully gone.

"Sure, I'll drive you home. I don't think it's a good idea if you drive." I scanned the statements she had given me. All three women had said the same thing. Three gunmen and no one saw the actual shooting. Perfect.

"No, thank you. I have to pick up Jason from my mom's house first."

The son.

I swallowed the lump in my throat and remembered what had put a screeching halt to my flirting with Emily. She had a kid. I was trying to come up with something to say or tamp down my irrational panic when Lenox spoke up.

"I'll drive you, Emily. Lily would have my balls in a sling if I let you drive. Considering we're trying for another baby, I sorta need them," he joked.

"Okay," she agreed.

That rankled. She told me no but would let Lenox take her to pick up her son. That's what I wanted, right? A way out. Lenox saved me by offering her a ride. I should've been happy she was safely getting home, and I didn't have to do it. But I was irked instead.

"Alright. I'll see you at the office, Lenox."

Lenox was right, there was something wrong with me. I needed to get the hell away from Emily and stop thinking about her. For the last six months, I have thought back to the day I met the raven-haired beauty and wondered what it was about her that calmed my ever-racing mind. We talked about nothing important or personal, not that I did that anyway, with anyone. She didn't overtly hit on me, but she did give as good as she got in the flirtation department. But it was different when she did it, she wasn't trying to be sexy to get me into bed. She was friendly and spirited. I had no idea why this woman got to me, but she did.

I was shocked when I saw her in the bank. I had been actively trying to avoid her. There had been two occasions I had turned down dinner at Lenox and Lily's house because I knew she'd be there. She was Lily's friend; that should've been enough to make her off-limits. But I couldn't stop thinking about her.

I pulled up to the hangar before Levi and parked my truck. I needed to get my head on straight and get laid. That had to be my problem. I hadn't had a woman in a very long time; it was hard to go back to easy pick-ups after meeting Emily. Fake and easy paled in comparison to her. I had to let the fantasy of her go and jump back into the saddle. No strings attached and mindless was all I deserved.

Easier said than done.

Levi and I were watching the bank footage when the Commander walked in. "Where's Lenox?"

"He took Emily home," I answered.

"Is Emily Jenkins going to be a problem?" he asked.

"Jenkins? As in Captain Jenkins?" I asked.

"One in the same."

Well, fuck me running. I knew Emily's husband was KIA, but I had never asked for her last name or details. I heard he had died with honor and bravely gave his life to save his rifle platoon.

"Emily is a non-issue. She's Lenox's wife's friend. That's all." Then why couldn't I get her out of my head?

"Good. Start the video over. I want to see when the first one walked in. What about the security cams from the dry cleaners next door?" the Commander asked.

"I downloaded the footage, they came in on foot. I checked all of the cameras from the surrounding buildings. I could trace them to the woods behind the barber. When they came out of the clearing, their masks were already on. Why not one person on the street gave them a second look is beyond me." Levi pointed to one of the monitors showing three men running out of the woods dressed in full battle gear.

"Well, I'll be fucked sideways. Why would anyone on an Army base that houses Rangers and an infantry battalion think twice about what looks like a regular training day? Are there cameras in those woods?" I asked Levi.

"Normally, yes. But the Ranger unit was training in those woods earlier in the week. They had new body armor and thermal imaging sights that they didn't want anyone to see. The cameras were disabled," Levi explained.

"Who knew about the cameras being disabled?" the Commander asked.

"It was need to know, but hard to say," Levi answered and fast forwarded to the injured robber fleeing the bank and running back into the woods. "How confident are you that your investigators can track those blood drops? Jasper clipped him in the bicep, and it was bleeding like a son-of-a-bitch. It should leave a nice trail if no one goes into those woods."

"I already called in Fink. She's my best CSI and has the best instincts and most importantly knows when discretion is necessary. Three perps that had access and knowledge. Someone's head is gonna roll for this." The Commander pulled a cigar out of a metal tube and bit the end off, spitting the nub into his palm. He tucked it into his pocket before he lit his cigar and gave it a few puffs. "Clark's still on leave. I'm sending you three in to pick up Roman's pilot. Lucky for you, ladies, he's down in Florida. It should be a day trip. And if Lenox bitches one more time about having to schedule missions around his wife's ovulation cycle, I'm cutting his balls off. No man that is worried about ovulation deserves to have a pair anyway."

We had kindly ridded the world of Roman last year. He was a traitorous asshole who sold out the U.S. for money. Selling weapons and munitions to any terrorist organization that would pay. Those weapons were used to kill U.S. service men and women. He was a scumbag of the highest order. The worst part about Roman was he used to be a part of the 707 before he defected. Before we killed him, he said he wasn't working alone. He had someone on the inside that was feeding him information.

"Why are we talking about my balls again?"

Lenox asked as he walked into the hangar. "Sounds like scrotum envy to me, Commander."

The Commander barked out a laugh. "Boy, I have bigger balls than you could ever hope to have."

Damn if that wasn't the truth. The Commander had a full rack of medals deploying to every major conflict since he enlisted. He was a serious badass.

"Do you really think the pilot knows anything?" I changed the subject from Lenox's balls. The truth was I didn't want to hear about either of their balls.

"He's our best lead to any intel Roman left behind. He murdered his staff before you caught up with him in the Bahamas. There was nothing at that location. Roman had to have stashed it somewhere," the commander explained, still puffing on his cigar. I choked back a cough and waved my hand in front of my face trying to dispel some of the thick smoke.

"What type of interrogation are we conducting?" I asked.

"A very clean one. We're stateside. If he proves to be difficult, maybe a few weeks in rendition will loosen his lips."

"Hopefully it doesn't come to that. I prefer not to work with the CIA," Levi said.

"The last time the spooks got involved they blew the op," Lenox added.

No one liked working with any outside agencies. Due to the secrecy of our ops, none of them knew our team existed. Which meant when we had to work with them they treated us like grunts instead of equals. Our chain of command was simple. The President gave his order to the Commander who in turn briefed us. That was it.

"When does our flight leave?" I asked.

The Commander looked at his watch. "Thirty minutes. I'll let you ladies get ready for your flight. Levi, I want that tape in the lockbox. No one views it without my okay."

"Copy that, sir."

Levi took the thumb drive out of his laptop and started shutting down his many computers. The Commander took off toward the door when he stopped and turned back to Lenox. "How's the boy?"

"Perfect. He's crawling now." Lenox's whole demeanor changed whenever he talked about his son. I was happy he and Lily had found their way back to each other and I could play a small part making sure they ended up together. Now their crazy asses were trying for another one when the first was only six months old.

"Glad to hear. Have a safe trip."

I was mentally calculating the time it would take

us to get to Florida, pick up the pilot, interrogate him, and ship him home. There was a constant nagging in my gut that something wasn't right. I didn't like that one of the robbers had escaped. I also didn't like that Emily and her son were left unprotected.

CHAPTER THREE

Emily

"Mom, I'm fine. Please stop before you scare Jason. I don't want him to know."

The last thing I wanted was my son knowing the bank was robbed. I was trying to come up with a way to spin the incident on the drive to my mom's – a way to downplay what had happened, but she took one look at me, and in true mama bear fashion, she knew something was wrong. It was on the tip of my tongue to try and lie when Lenox helpfully told her a watered down – what the Army wanted out - version of the story. It still wasn't enough to calm my mother. She was half crazy most days, give her something to worry about, and she was crazier than a loon.

"Emily Ann, someone tried to rob your bank today," she shrieked.

Yes, and held a gun to my head before he fell dead in front of me. I didn't say that last part out loud. My mom didn't need to know that, or she'd have a come apart for sure.

"I need to get Jason home and fed. Can you please drop me off at my house?"

I gave Lenox my car keys when he dropped me off, he said that he and the guys would drop off my car sometime tonight. All I really wanted to do now was get home, take a hot shower, and a cuddle with my boy.

"You can stay here tonight," my mom argued.

"No, mom. Please. I'm so tired."

After twenty minutes of back and forth, my mom finally relented and took us to my house – only after I threatened to call Uber. By the time we walked through the door, I was too tired to cook and declared it was pizza night, to which my awesome kid concurred. However, every night should be pizza night according to him. I ordered our food and plopped down on the couch next to Jason. He immediately scooted closer to me and burrowed into my side. I dreaded the day when he decided he was too old for this. Jason flipped through the channels trying to decide on a show. It didn't take long for me to replay today's events. Amazingly, I had held my shit together pretty well until the end when I saw the gun pointed at me, and I was certain I was going to die. It was days like these that I missed Steven even more than usual. I wished he was here to hold me. I was so scared today that I was going to leave Jason an orphan. I was still scared and barely holding on. If Steven were here, he'd know what to say to calm me down. He always had. From the first day I met him, I knew we'd always be friends.

Steven had a way about him that was both comforting and safe. He had picked me up when I was at my lowest point and helped me get my life together. I will always be grateful for the love and kindness he showed me. I missed him so much. I wished that Jason had gotten more time with him, too.

The knock at the door startled me pulling my attention back to the present. "Be right back buddy. Pizza's here."

By the time I got back to the living room, Jason had cleared off the coffee table to make room for the box. I didn't make a habit of letting Jason eat in front of the TV, but pizza night was the exception.

Jason spoke all the way through dinner about the

latest episode of his favorite shark series. Normally, listening to him prattle on was the best part of my day. But tonight, it did nothing to calm my frazzled nerves. The boy loved anything sea life. He could talk for hours about sea turtles and sharks — those were his favorite. Once he was yawning more than talking, I knew it was time for bed. The bank wouldn't be open tomorrow, but Jason had school and I needed to figure out if I wanted to continue to work at the bank after it reopened. I didn't think I could go back.

Maybe it was time for a career change. The bank was never meant to be permanent; it was simply a steady paycheck, a way for me to contribute to the household bills. Steven had insisted that it wasn't necessary, we could live comfortably on his officer's salary and Army benefits. But after all he had already done for me, I wanted to pitch in. It didn't seem right for me not to work.

"Mama, can I sleep with you tonight?" Jason asked when he was done brushing his teeth.

After Steven died, Jason slept in bed with me every night for almost a year. We both needed it. It was bittersweet when he started sleeping in his own bed again. It meant he was healing, but I missed having him close in my bed.

"Sure thing. Hop in, I'll be right there. But, no stealing the covers or I'll make you sleep in the bathtub."

Jason laughed at me as he climbed into my bed. "Would you really make me sleep in the tub?"

"Oh yeah. And I'd fill it with worms, too," I teased, giving a mock shudder.

"Mom, stop joking around. That's gross."

"Okay, I wouldn't make you sleep in the tub. I'd make you sleep in the dog house."

"We don't have a dog," he reminded me.

"Oh well, then you're safe."

"Can we get a dog? I'm old enough now. I can help. I would clean up after it," Jason begged.

Me and my big mouth. Why did I have to say anything about a dog house? So, so, dumb.

"We'll see," I answered, then for shock value I added, "you'll have to clean up all the poop from the backyard."

Jason's face scrunched up just like I knew it would. "That's so gross."

Ha! Maybe that will curb the puppy talk for a few more months.

Jason was fast asleep within minutes while I remained awake. My mind wouldn't shut off. I had a thousand things to figure out now. I could go a few months without working. However, I didn't want to dip too much into my savings. Steven's life insurance and death benefits were still sitting untouched in an account I was saving for Jason. I needed to find a new job, something I was passionate about.

It was after one a.m. when my phone chimed. I rolled to grab it off the nightstand to find a text message from Lenox. I was surprised he was here. Earlier tonight when Lily texted me, she said that the guys had a hiccup at the office and were more than likely having to pull an all-nighter to get the computers straight.

"Hey," I greeted when I opened the front door. "I didn't think you'd make it. Lily said a computer crashed or something."

"Or something," Lenox grumbled. "It was taken care of faster than we thought."

"Sorry to make you come all the way out here. I'm sure you want to get home." Movement behind Lenox caught my attention and Jasper came into full view.

What the hell was he doing here? After the way he left the bank today, I figured I'd never see him again. I thought I was doing the right thing letting him off the hook by declining his offer to drive me home. He had only offered to be nice. I remembered the way he reacted when he found out I had a son; his face went hard and all joking stopped. It was obvious he didn't like kids. I didn't hold it against him, even though it stung.

"It was no trouble at all. Hope we didn't wake you," Lenox said, offering me my keys.

"No. I was awake."

"Is everything okay?" Jasper asked coming to stand beside Lenox.

Why did the man look hotter every time I saw him? His hair was messy like he'd been running his hands through it in frustration. It was longer than the other guys'; he was pushing Army regs, which didn't surprise me at all. He didn't look like a man who liked to play by the rules. I could see him pushing and testing limits. The new scruff on his face made him look even sexier.

"Yea, everything's fine." I tried my best to smile. However, I must've failed because it had Jasper taking another step closer.

His smell assaulted my senses. Man and sweat, with a hint of smoke. I narrowed my eyes and wondered if they were really at the office. Jasper smelled more like a bar. I quickly dismissed the thought. Jasper might be a player, but there was no way that Lenox would ever lie to Lily. He was a good man, and I didn't really think Jasper would condone lying either.

"You sure? We could look around if you'd like," he offered.

"Look around? I'm fine. I was in bed going over my long to-do list. You know it's what us moms do. Plan and worry."

As if on cue, Jasper stepped back. It might've been a bitchy thing to do, using my son that way, but I was too tired to argue with Jasper. I figured he was used to getting his way, and I knew the mention of me being a mom would send him running for the hills.

"Alright. I hope you get some sleep." Jasper turned and walked down the driveway.

Wow. It was like I had a cool superpower. I could make Jasper disappear with one word.

"Listen, Emily, he doesn't..."

"It's fine. I don't take offense. He's a nice guy. Some people don't like kids. I'm cool with it."

"It's not like that. He just..." Lenox stumbled his words.

I cut Lenox off again. "It's not my business. It's fine really. He's never around when Jason and I are at your house. As long as he isn't mean to my son, everything will be fine. Besides, I'll probably never see him again." I offered Lenox a smile – a real one this time.

"I wouldn't bet on that," he said under his breath.

"Huh?"

"Nothing. If you ever need to talk about what happened today, Lily and I are here for you. The Army is trying to keep this under wraps until they finish their investigation. But you can talk freely to me or Lily," Lenox offered.

"Thanks. I'm fine," I lied.

"Try and get some sleep." Lenox waved and walked down the drive. He waited until I shut my door before he got in his car.

That night I fell asleep replaying Lenox's words in my head. *I wouldn't bet on it*. What did that even mean? Jasper ran every chance he got. I was the one with some weird fascination with the playboy, not the other way around. Jasper would be happy to never see me again.

CHAPTER FOUR

Jasper

It had been a week, yet here I was sitting in front of Emily's house again like a stalker. The first two days were to gather intel: what time her son got off the bus, what time she picked him up from her mom's, where she went grocery shopping, what stops she made, and finally what time the lights went out in her house. I thought I had her routine down when tonight a man showed up with flowers around dinner time. I hadn't expected that. Though I should've. She was a beautiful woman, why wouldn't she date? What bothered me, though, was the man was in her house with her son there.

It was none of my business, and I shouldn't have passed judgment, but I didn't like it. My gut was still screaming at me that something wasn't right. She was in danger. I still hadn't talked to Lenox about my suspicions. It would've thrown up red flags; he was the equivalent of a human lie detector and could smell bullshit a mile away. He'd ask questions I didn't want to answer. I could've told him I was only concerned because she was a nice girl and Lily's friend, but he'd see right through that. I couldn't get her out of my head. The last thing I wanted was my team knowing that. I've tried. Over the last week, I had scrolled through the numbers of hundreds of beautiful women who would jump at the chance to go another round. Yet, none of them were appealing. They only wanted what was on the surface, which was hypocritical of me to fault them for that because that was all I wanted from them. The crux of the issue was that none of them were her.

My heart came to a full stop when Emily's front door opened and she and her son stepped outside. Jason. Christ, the boy had a name, yet I couldn't get myself to use it. This wasn't the first time I'd seen the boy. I thought seeing him would get easier, but it hadn't. It didn't matter that I was attracted to her and felt some strange pull toward her. I had to put a stop to it. She deserved better, and I was a hundred percent sure that Jason deserved a man in his life who hadn't played a part in the death of his own child. I was surprised that Lenox and Lily allowed me in the same room with baby Carter. He was six months old, and I had yet to hold the kid. I was a complete asshole. I loved that they had a family. Hell, I was jealous. There was a time I wanted a wife and kids. Now, I whore around finding women who only want me for one thing – a good time. It's mutually beneficial for both, then I move on. No attachments, no hurt feelings.

The man hugged Emily and knelt in front of Jason pulling him into a hug, too. This must not be a first date then, or the guy is a total weirdo hugging the boy the first time he meets him. I didn't like him touching either one of them. What the hell was wrong with me?

THE LAST THREE Friday nights the same man had shown up at the same time. Only tonight he was late. Maybe they had broken up. Last week I promised myself that if he showed up again that next week, I wouldn't come to sit on Emily's house until after ten p.m. That's when he left. The third guy from the robbery still hadn't been found, and his identity was unknown. Every night I sat in front of Emily's house watching, making sure that she and Jason were safe. I was beginning to think that my gut was wrong; I was overreacting. Nothing had happened so far, and it had been a month since the robbery.

The team was getting ready to go out of the country, and as much as I didn't want to leave them unprotected, I felt a little bit better with each passing day.

A car pulled into Emily's driveway. Not Mr. Casanova that brought flowers each week. This was a piece of shit beater car. A man stepped out and looked around, his eyes landing on my car. The heavily tinted window provided me cover from him seeing in. *Yeah, you're being watched asshole.*

The man approached Emily's door and knocked. Emily opened the door and immediately tried to close it, but the man's hand shot out and caught the door before it could close.

I quickly folded out of the Camaro and jogged across the street. I wasn't silent in my approach. I wanted my presence known before the man could do anything stupid.

"Hey, sorry I'm late." I pushed past the man nudging his shoulder when I stepped around him. I heard him grunt as he pulled his right arm closer to his body.

"It's okay," Emily stammered.

She definitely didn't want this man on her porch if she was playing along. I cast a hard stare in the man's direction waiting for him say something.

"Hey man, what happened to your shoulder?" He was still holding his right arm. I'd had enough dislocated shoulders to know what that particular injury looked like.

"Nothing. Emily, I need to talk to you in private," he demanded.

"No, you don't. You need to leave. I have nothing to say to you." She shook her head for emphasis.

I could've easily removed the man right then and there, but I was hoping he'd say something that would explain Emily's behavior. When I wrapped my arm around her waist, she was shaking.

"I think you want to hear what I have to say to you." His brow lifted and a smile pulled up the corners of his mouth. "Why don't you step outside so we can talk in private?"

"Not gonna happen. She said she didn't want to talk to you." I stepped in.

"Mom, who's at the door?" Jason yelled from behind us. I scooted over so the man in front of us couldn't see into the house. No way I wanted him to get a look at the boy.

"That must be Jason." The man's smile got bigger.

"I didn't get your name," I prompted.

"None of your business. Last chance Emily."

"We're done here. And I don't ever want to see you come near Emily or her son."

"Is that a threat, soldier boy?" He laughed.

I let go of Emily and stepped closer to the man.

"Sure as fuck is. I hear you even breathe in their direction, it will be the last breath you ever take. And friend, that's not in the proverbial sense, I mean that literally. They do not exist to you."

"We'll see about that. You have something that belongs to me, Emily, and I'm back to collect. I'll admit, at least he's a step up from that..."

"I wouldn't finish that sentence. You do not disrespect her husband."

"Her husband. Yeah, okay. If that's the story she's telling." He laughed.

I stepped back into the house, pushed Emily back a step, and slammed the door.

"Who's this?" I heard a soft, shaky voice behind me.

Fuck, Jason. I inhaled trying to stop myself from

bolting out the door. At this point in time, I would've rather taken on fifteen Taliban warfighters than turn and face a six-year-old boy. What kind of pussy did that make me? The boy was scared, and as much as I actively tried to avoid any situation where I came into direct contact with children, I couldn't allow him to be scared.

"Jason, right?" I turned and stuck my hand out in a fist. "I'm Jasper."

Jason smiled and balled his little fist up giving mine a bump. "Yeah, I'm Jason."

"Cool. I came over to talk to your mom a minute. Sorry to barge in on you. Hope I'm not interrupting."

"No. Mom said it was bedtime," Jason groaned.

Emily still hadn't said anything. I wasn't sure what I was supposed to do. What do six-year-olds like to do? I needed Jason safely tucked away so I could talk to Emily alone.

"Have you seen the new Battlestar Empire game yet?" I asked pulling my phone out of my pocket. Kids liked video games, right?

"No. All my friends play it, but I don't have a phone to download it," he said. "Is it alright, Mom?" He looked at Emily with big hopeful eyes.

"Sure, honey," Emily mechanically answered.

I quickly disabled the messaging app and call

feature before handing it to Jason. "Why don't you play it in your room? You'll need the sound up," I suggested.

Jason looked at Emily when she nodded her head and took off to his room with my phone in hand.

I waited a few seconds before I turned to Emily. "Why don't we sit down?" I offered.

"You shouldn't be here," she angrily whispered.

Narrowing my eyes, I took in her defensive posture, and my hackles raised. "Why is that, Emily?"

"Why are you here? *How* are you here?" She asked, but didn't answer my question.

"I was driving by and thought I'd check in, see how you were doing."

"You were driving by? What? One of your women live in my neighborhood?" Was that jealousy I detected? And why did that please me so much? I didn't answer her. If I said yes, she'd shut down. If I told her the truth that there had not been a single woman since I met her at Lily's house, she'd likely call me a liar and kick me out.

"Let's sit. Who was at the door?" I asked.

Fresh tears fell from the corner of her pretty blue eyes.

"I can't. I don't want to talk about it. Everything's fine. You should go, just forget what happened."

Not so fast, sweetheart.

"That's not gonna happen. Nothing is fine. You're shaking like a leaf."

"I should get to Jason," she said, squaring her shoulders.

She obviously thought that if she reminded me about Jason, I'd run, just like every other time her son's name was mentioned. Not this time.

"Jason's fine." I smiled when her shoulders slumped forward.

She had no idea how long I could wait her out. I had all night to stand here.

"We have to leave." She frantically grabbed her purse and started for her cellphone on the coffee table. I grabbed her hand to stop her.

"Where are we going?" I asked.

"Not you. Me and Jason. We have to go."

"Calm down a minute. You need to tell me what's going on."

Emily plopped on the couch and covered her face with both hands and started to sob. She struggled against me when I sat next to her and pulled her to my chest. "Stop, Emily."

She finally settled in and allowed me to wrap my

arms around her. She felt good pressed up against my body, she felt right.

"I'm sorry," she cried and squeezed me tight. My heart pounded in my chest, and something clicked. I couldn't put a name to the emotion but feeling her holding onto me looking to me to offer protection and comfort did strange things to me.

"I am begging you to trust me. I can help you, but I need to know who that was, and why you are so afraid of him. I swear to you, you and Jason will be safe."

Self-doubt started to creep in. There was one other time in my life that I had begged. I begged God not to take Alesha from me. I couldn't stop my own child from dying, how could I promise Emily I could protect her and Jason? I had failed once before. I let Liz down, and Alesha was gone because of me and my shortcomings.

"Steven Jenkins was a good man," she started, only further reminding me that I couldn't be the man that Emily needed. Jenkins was a hero. I was a coward.

"Everything he did was to protect me and Jason. It was all my fault."

"Okay. I agree, but I'm not tracking."

I continued to wait until she finished her story.

"Steven's not Jason's biological father," she whispered. "I was pregnant when he married me."

That didn't explain why she had implied there was wrongdoing and it was her fault. Steven marrying her even though she was pregnant with another man's child only proved he was a good guy. Unless he didn't know.

"I knew Steven before he went into the Army. He was friends with my brother. Well, they were until my brother got involved with drugs. Steven distanced himself from Brian, but he'd still come around to check on me. Even after he went to college and enlisted. Every time he was home on leave he'd find me and make sure I was okay. The last time he… he found me…" Emily stopped and started to cry again. "He found me at my worst. Brian had OD'd, and I was lost, and lonely. I started dating one of Brian's friends. He was – not so nice to me."

"What do you mean, not so nice?" My blood boiled at the thought of someone hurting Emily.

"This is so embarrassing." Emily buried her face in my shirt and her hair fell curtaining her face. I gently brushed it away from her cheek and tucked the strands behind her ear.

"There's nothing for you to be embarrassed about. You did nothing wrong."

"Yes, I did. I stayed with him, even after he started hitting me. When Steven found me, I was pregnant and beaten. I was at my absolute bottom. Steven cleaned me up and went in search of Liam. When he came back a few hours later, his hands were cut up, and he told me I was leaving with him. When we got back to Georgia, he pulled up to the courthouse told me that as far as the world would know the baby was his, and he married me."

"Sounds like he loved you, and he did the right thing." I stroked her back for a few seconds knowing my next question was going to upset her. "I take it the man at the door was Liam?"

"Yes," she cried. "I haven't seen him since we left. He has never seen Jason. I didn't even know he knew where we were."

"Did he know you were pregnant when you left?" I asked.

"No. I had just found out. I only told Steven when we were driving to Georgia."

"Why did Liam say you have something of his, was he talking about Jason?"

"Yes."

"I don't understand. If he didn't know you were pregnant, why would he assume Jason was his. You were married to Steven," I asked.

Levi could easily falsify a DNA test to show Steven as Jason's father. It would be an easy fix to get Liam out of her life.

"Steven was gay."

"Come again?"

I didn't see that coming.

"Everyone back home knew he was gay. But he kept his private life well, private around here. Not because he was ashamed. Because he didn't want to be treated differently. He earned his commission, and he was a damn good and brave leader. He was afraid the men under him would think that he received some special treatment." I could understand that. Not that I cared one way or another, however, some people still did. "Steven gave up so much for me."

There was a knock at the door, and Emily all but flew off the couch. "Whoa. Everything's alright. Go back into the bedroom with Jason. I'll answer the door. And this time, don't come out until I give the all clear."

"No. It's alright. I'm sure it's Connor," she said.

Fuck. I forgot about the Friday night boyfriend. Well, too bad for Connor I wasn't leaving for their Friday night date, and the poor sucker's days were numbered.

"I'll still answer," I demanded, pulling my HK 45 from my concealed carry holster.

Emily didn't protest any further. Smart woman. I checked the peephole and sure enough, Mr. Friday night rose man was standing at the door.

I opened the door and almost laughed when Connor's smile turned into a deep frown.

"Is Emily home?" he asked.

"Sure is." I opened the door wider to reveal Emily standing beside me.

"Who are you?" he asked.

"Jasper," I answered offering no other information. I looked over his shoulder scanning the area for Liam which was easy considering I had a good six inches on the man in front of me.

"Would you like to come in?" I offered.

Now I was being a dick on purpose. Is this what being a petty, jealous asshole felt like? The concept of being jealous over a woman was foreign to me.

"Jasper!" Emily warned. "Hey Connor, I didn't think you were coming by tonight."

"Sorry, I should've called. I was done early." Connor made a weird grimace that had Emily laughing.

"That bad?" she asked.

"Dreadful. I can come another time if you're busy," he offered.

What man offers to come back later when he finds his woman with another man?

"Uncle Connor. You wanna see this cool new game that Jasper let me play?" Jason asked running into the living room.

"I do. But let me say hi to your mom first - and *Jasper*." Connor's tone changed when he said my name.

Uncle? Huh. That would explain why he offered to leave.

Jason ran back to his room, and Emily looked at me with one perfectly manicured eyebrow raised.

"Connor, this is my friend Jasper. You remember me telling you about my friend Lily? Jasper works with her husband, Lenox."

I didn't like the emphasis she put on the word *friend* before she said my name, and I certainly didn't like being introduced by association through Lily's husband.

That was going to have to change – on both accounts.

CHAPTER FIVE

Emily

This was awkward. How the hell was I going to explain who Connor was?

"Yes, I remember you mentioning Jasper," Connor answered.

I inwardly groaned at Connor's comment. I was going to kill him.

"She mentioned me?" Jasper's smug retort was accompanied with a sly smile.

"She sure did. I know all about how you bolt at the mention of Jason's name." Hurt flashed in Jasper's eyes before he recovered and quickly masked it.

Now, I was really going to kill him. "Connor, can I talk to you in the kitchen?"

"You could, or we can talk in front of Jasper since he and I need to have a little chat anyway. Why are your eyes red? You look like you have been crying." Connor turned to Jasper narrowing his eyes. "And why is a man who by all accounts has an allergic reaction to kids in your house? On alert, no less." Connor stopped again to face me. "You allowed him to answer your door, and when he did, his hand was still hovering over his sidearm. Which tells me, he's a smart man not trusting me when I walked in even if you said you knew me. He didn't stand down until Jason confirmed he was comfortable with me being in the house."

"Was there a question in there?" I tried to deflect.

"How much do you know?" Jasper ignored me and addressed Connor.

"I'd like to say everything, but the Army is keeping a lid on the robbery. Even with my connections, there's a lot redacted," Connor answered. "I pieced most of it together, but there's some conjecture on my part."

Wait! What was going on?

"And your connections are?" Jasper asked.

"I think maybe..." I tried to interject.

"The jig is up, sweetheart. Time to start talking," Connor interrupted me.

"The jig? Who says that?" I asked, and Jasper growled in impatience. "Did you growl at me? Does that work for you?"

"I don't know, I've never done it before. Probably because I've never cared about a woman enough to wade into a situation that directly affects her safety and well-being," he answered.

What! Did he say care about a woman? As in he cared about me?

"Deputy Connor O'Brien, US Marshal Service," Connor told Jasper.

"What do you have on Liam?" Jasper asked Connor, but his eyes never left mine.

I thought I might throw up. My past was coming back to haunt me. I never thought I would see or hear from Liam again. We needed to move. I had to call my mom and tell her to start packing. Which was going to suck for her. She just moved here to help me with Jason a year ago.

"Street thug in Petersburg, about eight hours north of here. Low-level dealer. His crew is known for armed robberies and petty B and E's. Are you thinking..." Connor trailed off.

"Considering he showed up here about an hour

ago and you just told me his crew runs armed robberies, a bank heist isn't a far stretch. I'm thinking there's a strong possibility. I don't believe in coincidences."

There was no way that Liam could plan a bank robbery. He was too dumb. Most the time he was too high to string two sentences together.

Connor's face turned to stone. "How'd you know he was here?"

"I've been sitting on her house since the night of the robbery," Jasper told him.

"You what?" I asked.

"The Camaro? I ran the plates. They came back with a registration to the house next door."

Jasper smiled. "Nifty little trick."

"You what?" I repeated.

Both men looked at me like they had forgotten I was even standing here.

"I've been parked in front of your house every night since the day of the robbery," Jasper said.

"That was a month ago. You've been sleeping in your car in front of my house? Why?"

"No, Emily. I have not been sleeping, I've been watching, making sure you and Jason are safe. As to the why, because I didn't like that the third man in the robbery got away. Something didn't feel right. In my line of work, if something doesn't feel right, it's not. I trust my gut, always. Tonight, it paid off, and I was across the street and able to get to you before Liam could push his way into your house."

"In your line of work? You audit gear and stuff."

I was so confused. Why would Jasper sit in his car for a whole month and watch my house? He barely knew me. Why not tell Lenox? At least he was my friend.

"Sweetheart, if you've been buying that line of shit, you need to open your eyes. Does this man look like he sits behind a desk all day and checks in gear?" Connor laughed. "If I had to guess, I'd say Special Forces. Though black ops wouldn't be a far stretch." He gave Jasper an appreciative once-over. That was something both men had in common; they were shameless flirts. Only they batted for different teams.

"Jasper, your phone just beeped. I think I ran down your battery." Jason joined us in the living room and handed Jasper back his phone.

"Thanks, bud. Did you like the game?" Jasper asked.

I couldn't believe that he was in my house and talking to my son.

"It was totally awesome. Do you think I could play it again?"

"I don't think..." I started.

"Of course you can." Jasper gave Jason another fist bump.

"Cool."

No. That was *not* cool. I was okay with Jasper not wanting to be around me because I had a child. What I was not cool with was Jasper implying to Jason he'd be back, even though we both knew he wouldn't be. As soon as this robbery thing was taken care of, Jasper would go back to being allergic, using Connor's word, to kids.

"Hey, Jason, it's time to brush your teeth."

"Okay, but can I talk to Uncle Connor before I go to bed?"

"You go brush up, and I'll be back to tuck you in, in just a minute." Connor smiled at Jason.

I loved how close Connor was to Jason. We were not a conventional family. Hell, most would've found our arrangement twisted, but it worked for us. The most important thing was, we all loved each other.

Jasper was fiddling with his phone, and I tried to get Connor's attention. But he was ignoring me or pretending to.

Finally, Jasper put his phone to his ear. "I'm at Emily's. Negative. Whatcha got on a Liam? Fuck, hold on." Jasper looked at Connor. "Liam Gains?" he asked.

This could not be good. How did the person on the other end of the phone come up with Liam's last name so fast?

"Yes," Connor answered, his tone mirroring my thoughts.

"Did you hear that…yes…we have a bigger problem. Negative, I'm not leaving Emily's house. I need you to come to me. The Camaro's parked out front, track that for the address – no need to get Lenox out of bed this late. I need you and Clark here ASAP. And one more thing before you come. Pull a Deputy Connor O'Brien US Marshal Service. Full work up. If he checks out, get a blue badge for him from the Commander… Copy that, see you in ten." Jasper swiped his phone and placed it in his pocket. "Sorry about that man, protocol."

Connor didn't answer but nodded in understanding. "I'm gonna go tuck Jason in."

"What just happened?" I asked.

"I need you to listen to me very carefully Emily. In about ten minutes, you are going to see and hear things that you cannot ever repeat. I wish there was another way, but I'm not leaving you here unprotected, and it looks like I'm going to need Connor's help."

"I don't understand," I answered him.

"Which part?"

"All of it, or none of it." Jasper stood in front of me almost willing me to see him. I looked at him with new eyes, forgetting everything Lily told me about Lenox and what the guys did. The way Jasper stood, his posture, the way he carried himself. I thought back to how he handled the robbery, the ease with which he took control of the situation. I didn't have to see him fire the gun to know he killed those men. He saved my life. "You don't really check in gear, do you?"

"No, sweetheart, I don't."

"You saved me. That man was going to kill me. He had...he had his gun pointed at my head. All I could think about was how I was going to die and leave Jason."

Jasper wrapped his strong arms around me and let me cry into his chest.

My life was crumbling around me, and the only thing that was keeping me standing was Jasper.

CHAPTER SIX

Jasper

I held Emily in my arms while she cried and once again noted how perfect she felt pressed against me. The internal war continued to rage; my head knew I couldn't pursue her, but every other part of me was screaming to keep her. I looked over her head to find Connor staring at us, his expression hard.

My phone vibrated in my pocket, and I pulled it out, carefully unlocking it one-handed. Levi and Clark were already outside, and they were doing a perimeter sweep.

"Em. The guys are here," I whispered into her hair. She nodded against my chest. In a moment of weakness, I kissed the top of her head. Need outweighed logic.

"I don't know what I'm supposed to do," she spoke into my chest and held on tighter.

"Why don't you go lie down with Jason while Connor and I talk to the guys?" I suggested.

"I'm scared."

"You're safe here. We are going to work on a plan to get Liam out of your life for good. Jason will be safe. He won't touch either of you."

Her bloodshot eyes came up to meet mine. "Why are you doing this?" she asked.

I brushed her hair over her shoulder exposing her neck and ear and leaned in close. "I can't explain the why. I only know that there's something inside of me that won't let me walk away from you. You're under my skin, and no matter how hard I've tried the last seven months, I can't work you out. I'm fucked up, Emily. Honestly, you should be pushing me away right now. But I have to say, I'm pleased as fuck you're not. I promise you I'll do my best to keep you both safe."

She pulled away and looked up at me, and in a moment of clarity, I realized how Emily had wormed her way in. When Emily looked at me, she saw *me*. She didn't bat fake eyelashes to get my attention, she didn't purse her lips to try and look sexy. She locked eyes and didn't let go. She didn't let me hide. Her gaze was searching, and as hard as I tried, I couldn't deny her. Yet, I had to try and find a way to break her spell. She was a mom, and I had lost my chance at being a dad.

"I know you will." She stood up on her tiptoes and kissed my cheek before she turned and walked toward the bedroom.

I didn't have to hear Clark and Levi to know they were in the room; I felt their presence the moment they had entered the house. I knew all eyes were on me. My team had watched me successfully hit on and take home a lot of women, yet none of them had ever seen me holding a woman.

"What did you find?" I asked Levi.

My hopes of diving right into work went straight to hell when I turned to find both men staring at me. By the expressions on their faces, their mouths might as well have been hanging open.

"Go ahead, spit it out. We have shit to do," I encouraged. They were going to ask, might as well get it out of the way.

"I got nothing to say," Levi wisely said.

"'Bout goddamn time you pulled your head out of your ass," Clark grumbled.

I glanced at Connor. He looked like he had

plenty to say. His jaw was tight, and the vein in his neck was throbbing.

"In the interest of time and full disclosure, she talks about you, a lot. All of you; however, her eyes light up and she gets this look when she talks about you. I looked into you. It took a while to get a lock, but I did. Your service record was what I thought it would be – bullshit. The Army has put out only what they want someone to find. I was more concerned with your past. I want you to know I will not give them up without a fight."

"The fuck?" My body locked tight and was coiled ready to strike. If a fight's what he was after he had stepped up to the right man.

"Calm down." Connor put his hand up only further pissing me off. "They are all I have left. We lost Steven eighteen months ago, and you are the first man in six years who has caught her attention. She knows you're not interested in her. She plays it off that she's okay you don't like kids and you're not interested in her, but I see the pain she tries to hide. That woman is an open book. What you see, is what you get. The man who ends up with her and Jason is one lucky son-of-a-bitch."

"What did you say? Six years? I would hope she

wasn't interested in other men when she was married." This from Levi.

The situation was damn complicated; Levi and Clark didn't know about Steven and the reasons he and Emily got married. And I really didn't like my personal life being aired, not to mention that Connor was right the man who got Emily would be lucky. I just didn't deserve to be that man.

"As much as I want to tell you that Emily's personal life isn't up for discussion, unfortunately, you'll need the background."

I told Levi and Clark the story about Liam and why Steven married her. I also filled them in on me sitting on Emily's house for the past month. I think the guys were more shocked and a little pissed I had been staking out her house without telling them than they were about Steven and Emily's fake marriage.

"And where do you fit into this?" Levi asked pulling a folder out of his backpack handing it to me. "I did a full work up on you as well." He wasn't all that pleased either that Connor had done a background check on me. I knew I was clean and my service records were sealed. But I also knew what he did find. My daughter's death certificate. The thought that he knew about my daughter had me seeing red.

"A friend," Connor replied.

"What kind of friend?" Levi pushed.

I didn't understand where Levi was going with this; however, if he was pushing it meant he knew something.

"A close one." Connor didn't seem to like being on the receiving end of being questioned.

"We can do this all night. I read your jacket, you seem like a smart guy. The fact that we are standing here and Jasper asked me to get clearance for you from the Commander means you gotta know my authorization to access intel has no limits. I'm not asking to judge you, what I'm really after is does Emily know. You are squeaky clean on paper. Personally, I care more about a man's morality than I do how he handles his cases."

Levi's the most laid back and quiet of the bunch, he's also the one that does not trust men easily. We are all skeptical of outsiders. Though, Levi takes it to a whole new level.

"Yes, she knew. Steven and I had been seeing each other for over a year when he brought Emily to Georgia. At first, I was furious, hurt, and I felt betrayed. I was very much in love with him. I broke it off with him, but it was Emily that found me and begged me not to leave Steven. She said that nothing would change." Connor stopped to regain his composure. "Yet, everything did. I didn't think I could love him any more than I already did. I was wrong; talking with Emily and her telling me everything that had happened and what Steven was doing for her proved what a good person he was. It wasn't just me and Steven anymore. We had Emily, too. And then we had Jason. I was Uncle Connor, and Steven was Daddy. I love them all, they are my family."

Say what? It took a minute for me to wrap my head around what Connor had said. He and Steven were lovers? And Emily knew? What about Emily, was she with other men? Were they... did they...?

"I see you're trying to work everything out. To answer one of the questions swirling around, no, the three of us were never together like that. Steven and I were exclusive with each other and very much gay, not bisexual. And no, Emily had not looked at another man, let alone dated. Steven did try, though."

Thank fuck. I didn't know if I'd be able to handle knowing that Emily had been with Connor. Which was comical considering my sexual past. I shouldn't have been thinking about anything to do with sex when it came to her; I was trying to put distance between us.

"The Commander gave clearance," Levi announced as if Connor hadn't just spilled his personal secrets to us. That was Levi's way. Direct and to the point. When he got an acceptable answer he found to be the truth, he moved on.

None of us cared about his or Steven's sexual preference, and as unconventional as their arrangement was, if everything was on the up and up no one cared about that either.

Levi pulled four more folders out of his backpack and laid them on the kitchen table. Clark was still silently watching – he knew something. After all the years we had worked together I could read him; I knew all his tells, and the ticking in his jaw was a dead giveaway.

"Keith Lands, E2 mechanized unit." Levi pointed to one of the folders. "He was the douchebag whose neck was snapped. A few small infractions, nothing to write home about." Levi pointed to the next folder. "Jeff Miller, E4 same unit, douchebag that took a bullet to the head. He was in the process of being article fifteened out. Seems he thought it would be a good idea to run coke out of his barracks room. Why wasn't he in the brig you ask? He was selling a ton of the shit to Officer Phillips. After the MPs locked Miller's room down waiting for the local narcotics detective to come, Phillips happened into Miller's room. The two keys. Yes, ladies you heard correct, the two keys went missing."

"Did you pull Phillips' financial?" Connor asked.

I opened Miller's folder, he was obviously the idiot who planned the bank robbery. He was an average-at-best solider. No commendations, no deployments. Nothing interesting, I opened Phillips' folder.

"I did. He had regular wire transfer into an account; small weekly amounts that would never set off any red flags. They stopped approximately fifteen months ago."

"Any connection to Roman?" Clark asked, taking the words out of my mouth.

Before we killed Roman, he said he was working with someone. When we questioned Roman's pilot, he proved to be a dead end. We spent three hours with the man, and during that time, he was willing to spill every secret he knew, that was in between him pissing his pants and crying. Roman was smart. There was no way that Roman would trust a sniveling moron with important information. We were back to square one. As much as we would like to spend all of our time tracking down the traitor, if there was one, scumbags didn't take timeouts and we'd be called back to the field soon. We were almost out of time.

"There's a loose connection. I'm still digging," Levi explained.

"Liam Gains? Where does he fit in?" I asked.

"We ran a bloody print from when you clipped him. Shitty shot by the way." I flipped Levi the bird. "After he was shot, he ran back into the woods and took his gloves off. He touched the metal chain link fence post before he crawled through the opening they had cut. His prints are in the system. Surprisingly as a confidential informant."

Clark eyed Connor. There was the missing piece that had Clark on edge. He hated loose ends.

"That come from your office?" Clark asked.

"Hell no. I have two CIs I work, both I keep in my back pocket and off any records you'll find, and I have them because they have mob ties. I don't fuck with petty theft bullshit. If he wasn't in WITSEC, it didn't come from us."

"Maccino and Luci," Clark said, and Connor's face paled. "There's no such thing as *off record*."

Now Clark was just showing off. It was true, there was no information we couldn't access.

"I'd appreciate you keeping those names to yourself," Connor grumbled.

"The same way that everything you see and hear is off the record?"

"Copy that," Connor acknowledged.

Leverage.

Clark had found what he needed to ease his mind that Connor wouldn't talk. There was no doubt I was pissed as hell at Connor for invading my privacy, but the man struck me as loyal.

"Let me guess, Gains was supplying the coke to Miller. Miller lost the product and needed to pay Gains back. Gains, not trusting Miller to not take off with the money, came down here to oversee the robbery. Now the question is did Gains know that Emily and Jason lived here and that she worked at the bank?"

"Doubtful. Gains is an out of sight, out of mind kinda guy. I'll look into it and find out why he's in the system as a CI. What did he say to her tonight?" Connor asked.

I told Connor, Clark, and Levi what Liam said.

"He's not here for Jason," Connor said. "Emily probably doesn't even remember, but when she left Liam, she brought what looked to be an address book with her. She was going to toss the book, but Steven took it. There are no telephone numbers in the book but there are groupings of random numbers. He doesn't know that Jason is his. She's scared, and when you have a secret, you're paranoid that others know it, too. I guarantee he wants that book back."

"Where's the book?" Clark asked.

"In my safe, at home," Connor answered.

Shit, if Liam wanted the book bad enough, God knows what he'd do to get it back.

"It's late. Thanks for coming by. Let's meet up at the hangar in the morning," I suggested.

"Copy. Here, you'll need this." Clark handed Connor a gate pass and blue badge that would allow him access to the building. "We'll meet you there at ten hundred and take you back to the hangar with us. See what you can dig up on Gains, and we'll work on Phillips." Clark turned his eagle eye toward me. "You good?"

No. Warning bells were going off all over the place.

"Five by five," I lied. Clark didn't budge. Is this what Lenox felt like when we cornered him about Lily? "I'm good. Keeping Emily and Jason safe is the only thing taking up headspace at the moment."

"You'll let me know if it gets to be too much." That was not a request on his part. "O'Brien, appreciate your help on this. We'll see you in the morning."

"I'll leave these here for you to go over. I assume you'll be in the Camaro all night," Levi said.

"You assumed right."

"I'll stay. You can go home," Connor offered.

"I'll be in the Camaro."

"You two work out whose dick is bigger, I'm out of here." Clark laughed and headed for the front door, Levi following behind.

The door closed and Connor was picking up his coat. "Does she know?"

My eyes closed and my heart constricted. "No."

"I read the report about Alesha. I understand your reaction to Jason. When you're ready, you should tell her. She'd understand, too. Clearly, there's something between you two. I know how she feels. I had doubts about you, still do, only because I don't think you'll man up and let yourself be happy. I see the way you look at her, I saw how you were comforting her. I believed you when you promised to keep them safe. Do me one favor, while you're working your shit out, don't hurt her. And do not make promises to that boy that you can't keep." Connor put his jacket on while I was counting to ten trying to calm down before I beat his ass. He made his way to the front door and stopped. "Take the couch, it's more comfortable than the car. And thanks for saving her."

With that, he walked out the door leaving me seething mad and speechless. Not an easy feat. Who the fuck did he think he was? Man up?

Fuck!

The worst part was he might be right.

Emily

The smell of coffee roused me from sleep. It took me a minute to realize I was in Jason's bed – alone. Where was Jason? As if on demand, his laugh floated into the bedroom filling me with a warmth only my son could. Last night when I fell asleep sometime after one, I still heard voices in the living room and figured Connor would come back and wake me up before he left. He must've spent the night, he'd never leave without saying goodbye. The brewing coffee was another indication he'd stayed over. I never remembered to program that damn thing.

Bless him! If there was ever a morning I needed a cup of his thick mud-like coffee, it was this morning.

I jumped out of bed, not bothering to brush my

teeth or check myself in the mirror, I needed coffee that bad.

"I think I love you," I announced when I walked down the hall toward the kitchen. "You are quite possibly the world's best man."

Yawning, I pulled the hair tie off my wrist and started to pile my long black hair on top of my head in a messy excuse for a ponytail.

"And you haven't even tried my pancakes yet." A male voice that was most definitely not Connor's said from beside me causing me to jump in surprise. "Mother fu... damn, that's hot," he cursed.

I dropped my arms, abandoning my ponytail in an effort to regain my footing. I felt the telltale sting of a sharp Lego on the bottom of my foot and lost my balance, hitting my hip on the arm of the couch on the way down.

"Christ, woman! Are you okay?"

Nope. I wasn't okay, not even a little bit. There I sat on my floor with my eyes closed, utterly humiliated.

When I braved to peek out my squinted eyes, a pair of perfect male feet stood in a puddle of spilled coffee. I hated feet, yet I couldn't stop staring at his.

"Let me help you up," Jasper said. "Careful, the coffee's hot."

I felt my cheeks pinken at my wild imagination; I had thought for the briefest of seconds he was calling me *hot*. Now that I saw the large coffee stain down the front of his tee and the puddle on the floor, I realized he was talking about the hot liquid. I took his outstretched hand and wasn't sure if I was going to punch him for scaring me half to death or if I wanted to run and hide in the bedroom. All thoughts of bodily harm fled my mind when his hand wrapped around mine and he yanked me up. The first thing I noticed was how warm his hand was, the second was how much bigger it was than mine, and finally but certainly not least, I felt a pulse of electricity pass between us.

"I'm sorry, I didn't mean to scare you," he murmured.

"Why are you here?" I asked.

With his free hand, he brushed my half tied up hair off my face. Was it my imagination or had he let his hand brush my neck on purpose? I couldn't think clearly with him standing close enough that I could smell the coffee on his breath. Who was I trying to bullshit? I couldn't think straight when he was in the same room, close or not.

"It was late when Connor and the guys left.

Connor said you wouldn't mind if I stayed on your couch instead of the Camaro."

I still didn't understand why he was doing any of this. Don't get me wrong, I was grateful that he was there last night when Liam showed up. I don't know what I would've done if he'd pushed in and taken Jason.

"Hey, look at me," he said. "Everything will be okay."

"Hi, Mom. Good Morning." Jason's chipper voice saved me from further thinking about the shitty situation I now found myself in.

"Hey, sweet cheeks," I greeted.

"Come on, you have to try some of Jasper's blueberry pancakes. They're the best. He taught me his secret ingredient," Jason informed me.

"He did? What is it?" I asked.

"I can't tell you. It's top-secret. Jasper said that means it's a super-duper important secret. Hurry up, there's only three left." By the way Jason was bouncing back into the kitchen, I'd guess the top-secret ingredient was sugar, and lots of it.

"He's right, they are pretty damn good. You better hurry, he's already had about a dozen." He tugged my hand signaling for me to follow and glanced at where our hands were still connected.

Even his hand was sexy, rough and strong. He had to leave. I couldn't do this, not this early in the morning. Not when my brain was pre-coffee and fuzzy. I needed to secure my armor and prepare for the battle that was Liam. I had a lot to explain to my mom, and Connor would be bummed we were leaving Georgia. There wasn't much left for us here anyway now that Steven was gone. Although I was going to miss Lily and baby Carter. I loved that little boy. Every time I was over there it made me think about how badly I wanted another child.

"Well, I don't know what to say? Thank you for making him pancakes. I'm sure you'd like to go and get ready for work. I've got it from here." I pulled my hand free from his, expecting relief to cross his face.

Instead, I got his stormy blue eyes zeroing in on me and a not so relieved expression. "You've got it from here?" he asked.

"Yeah. Thank you so much for your help last night and for watching us. Now that you know who the third robber is, I bet you'll be happy to get home into your bed at night." I smiled trying to show him how much I truly did appreciate all he had done.

"You've got to be shitting me," he mumbled.

"What? I really truly appreciate everything." I tried again.

"What part of this situation are you not understanding?" he asked.

I didn't appreciate his tone or his insinuation that I was somehow dumb and didn't understand this was serious.

"I understand this situation just fine, thank you very much. I'm not some mindless twit. I plan on dropping Jason at school and then stopping by my mom's to tell her that Jason and I are moving. I can't live here anymore now that Liam knows where we are. I won't take any chances with my son."

Jasper's eyes narrowed and his scowl deepened. "You're doing what?" I started to repeat myself when his hand came up to stop me. "You're not moving anywhere," he told me.

"Um, yes, I am. I'm not safe here," I reminded him.

Now who didn't understand the seriousness of the situation? Not to mention, why did he care?

"That's exactly why you have to stay. You're not safe. What if Liam follows you or finds you again? You need to be here where I can protect you."

"What, are you going to sleep outside my house every night?"

"If I have to," he assured me.

"That's ridiculous. You can't sleep in your car. What if he doesn't come back for a while?"

"I've slept in worse places. Unless you have a better offer," he said with a wink.

Luckily Jason ran past us reminding me I had to get him to school. I didn't have time to think about the tingling Jasper's wink caused in my girly parts.

"I need to get going. Jason needs to get to school," I told him hoping he'd get the hint and leave.

"I'll drive you there. We need to talk to the school, too," he informed me.

"What? Who is *we*?"

Now what was he talking about? I needed to call Connor; he'd fill me in on what happened last night.

"Me and you. We need to go over safety protocols with the school. We also need to show them a picture of Liam. If he shows up at the school, they'll know to call the police," he explained.

"You think he'll go to Jason's school?" Panic started to bubble up. Why hadn't I thought of that? Oh, yeah, I remembered why. My brain got foggy and I turned stupid every time I was around Jasper. I seemed to have memory lapses as well. "You should leave," I told him again, this time with conviction behind my words.

"Why's that, Emily?" he demanded, his tone matching mine.

"Because I can't think when you're around. And besides..." I lowered my voice to a whisper. "I get that being around kids really isn't your thing. Again, thank you for making him breakfast even though I'm not entirely sure why you did it."

Jasper stood silently staring at me, his look somewhere between pissed and amused. I tamped down the desire to give him the hand gesture to move along. I know I had another stop to make on what was an already long list of places I needed to be.

Jasper looked as if he wasn't going to move. Fine, he could stay here. "I have to leave. Please lock the door when you go." I turned to go get dressed when Jasper grabbed my arm to stop me. "I'm late. I still have to..."

"Be quiet." He spoke through clenched teeth.

"Excuse me? Who the hell..."

He cut me off again. "Do I think I am?" He finished my sentence. "If you'd cool your jets for two seconds and let me talk, I'll explain. You are not gallivanting around town unprotected. We'll take Jason to school, then we'll go to my house so I can shower and change. We are meeting up with my team at ten. When we're done there, we will go pick up Jason from school and come back here. As to the *who the hell do I think I am?* I am the man who is going to make sure that Liam Gains does not fuck with you or Jason. The why? Because for seven months, I have tried everything in my power to push you out of my mind. Nothing has worked. Time to change tactics and find out what about you has me tied in knots. And just for the record, I like that you can't think when you're around me."

I will admit, there was a small sliver of hope and a whole lot of excitement that welled in my chest. But it quickly waned. I was a mom; I didn't have time for hope and excitement. Besides, nothing had changed.

"I'm not some mission. You don't get to fall back and regroup. I don't have time for games."

"I don't play games, Emily. You are not a game to me," he vowed, his face was firm, void of his normal playfulness.

"I believe you think you mean that. But I can't take the chance with Jason. If it were just me, hearing you say I've tied you in knots would make me want to jump for joy. And that's embarrassing to admit, but the truth. I have to think about Jason," I reminded him.

He didn't stop me when I walked away, only

further solidifying I made the right choice. Not that he gave me options, only an implication that there might be something between us. Something I wished I could explore. Jasper was the first man in more than six years who with nothing more than a few mundane conversations stirred my interest. There was so much more to Jasper than he let the world see. The woman who put the time in to break him down would hit pay dirt when he opened up.

What was the saying? Right guy, wrong time.

In another life....

CHAPTER EIGHT

Jasper

Emily was cute when she pitched a hissy fit. I think she might've actually stomped her foot when she saw me waiting with Jason by the front door. I know she slammed the passenger door of the Camaro when I insisted I drive, and Jason declared that my black sports car was the coolest thing he'd ever ridden in. She may even have hissed when I told her I was going into the school to explain the situation to the administration.

Being that the school was full of Army families, security was pretty tight. One of the dads was an ex-Ranger who headed up a group called Watch Dogs. The D-O-G stood for Dads On Guard. Each dad took a day to volunteer at school and walk the halls helping wherever they were needed. They also handled visitor passes and walked the perimeter of the school grounds. With minimal detail, I explained the situation, leaving out who Liam Gains really was. The man on duty that day was more than happy to help and would brief the rest of the dads.

Now we were back in the car, and Emily was pouting. I had refused to take her to her mom's so she could tell her she was moving.

"Two reasons, Emily. One, you're not moving. Two, if Liam Gains doesn't already know where your mom lives, I'm not taking a chance by leading him there."

"Is she in danger, too?"

I wanted to tell her that every person she had ever met might be in danger, but I refrained. Mostly because it was a slight exaggeration and that statement might send the woman over the edge.

"I texted Connor and asked him if he had any buddies on the force. He said he knew a few local guys and called in a favor. There will be frequent drive-bys at your mom's. She'll be fine," I explained.

I might've failed to mention that I knew a security guy who owed me a favor and he was over there now installing a new alarm system. When he was done there, he was going to Emily's to update hers. The system she had now was shit and only alerted the low budget company that serviced it. There was no way in hell I was trusting a rent-a-cop with her safety.

"Thank you," she conceded.

"You're welcome. While you're already in a snit, I should probably tell you a few more things," I started.

"I'm not in a snit!"

"Then you always walk around slamming shit and mumbling under your breath? I think I heard you say dick a few times. Just so you know, the offer's on the table if you'd like mine." I tried to joke to lighten the mood.

"Is that how this works?" she asked.

"What works?"

"You offer a woman your dick, and she jumps at the chance to have the famous Jasper for a week?"

I wanted to roll my eyes and tell her that I didn't even have to offer. But I thought better of it. The truth was I had known one day my whoring ways would catch up with me. I just didn't think it would make me feel like such a dirty asshole when they did.

"I wouldn't believe everything you hear."

"So, it's not true? You don't toss women aside after a week?" she pushed.

"You really want to do this?"

"Yes," she confirmed.

"Do you have questions or you want me to just explain?"

"Why a week?" She twisted in her seat, and I could feel her gaze settle on me.

"Because feelings don't develop in a week. I was always clear and upfront about what I was willing to give," I answered.

"What's wrong with developing feelings?"

Holy fuck, I would rather be in an interrogation room full of men threatening to pull out my fingernails.

"Nothing. If that's what you're after. I wasn't."

We stopped at a red light, and I looked over at her, I could practically hear the gears turning in her head.

"Why don't you like kids? Or is it just Jason?"

The ever-present ache in my chest rose to the surface and promised to choke me. This was a bad idea; she had asked the one question that was off limits.

"It's not Jason."

"I'm sorry, that was really rude of me to ask," she whispered.

"But asking me about my sex life isn't?" I snapped.

"You're right, it is. And it's none of my business."

Emily turned forward, and I instantly missed the warmth of her stare.

"Listen, the truth is, I never wanted a relationship. I didn't want to be tied down to one woman. My job takes me away a lot. I've seen a lot of relationships and marriages break up because of deployments. In my job, I have to be a hundred percent focused. I can't be worrying if my woman back home is out running around on me. This might make me sound like a dick, but if a woman is quick to throw herself at me, she'll do it behind my back when I'm gone. If I limit my interactions to a week, no one gets hurt."

"Okay." She still sounded dejected.

"I'm sorry. I didn't mean to snap at you. I've never had to explain my sexual past to anyone. I'm sure you can tell I'm not very good in the communication-with-a-woman department. Finish your questions," I offered.

"Aren't you lonely?" she continued her questioning.

"Yea," I admitted.

I don't think I've ever admitted that to another

soul. I couldn't remember the last time I held a woman and enjoyed the weight of her in my arms or laid in bed and kissed just to kiss.

"I'm sorry. I know what it feels like to be surrounded by people and still feel lonely. Steven was a great friend, he was attentive, and we always had fun, but at the end of the day he went to his room, and I went to mine. Most weekends he would spend with Connor if he was in town. They always included us in their plans. But I was the outsider. It was always just me and Jason..." she trailed off.

"Don't do that." I sighed. "Don't not talk about Jason because you think it will make me uncomfortable. He's a great kid. Please, Emily, I'm asking you to trust me and give me some time. I might be an ass, but I am not a liar."

"I love my son," she continued. "But I miss the feel of a man pressed against me. I miss someone touching me and kissing me. Do you know I haven't kissed a man in almost seven years?"

Just hearing her say those words had my dick stirring to life.

"Seven years, Jasper. I'm a born-again virgin. I don't even remember what sex feels like."

I had so much I wanted to say in response to that, like, I would happily take her born-again virginity and remind her of all the ways a man could and should be touching her body. I also wanted to tell her that it wouldn't be just any man who was going to take her, it was going to be me. However, we had pulled up to the guard gate to enter the base, and I had an erection to beat into submission. I tried to adjust my dick in my jeans so I could get my wallet out of my back pocket without snapping it in half. When she caught me, her eyes widened and her cheeks blushed.

"What can I say? Hearing you talk about wanting a man to touch you is sexy as hell." Maybe she thought I was embarrassed she caught me, but I wasn't. I couldn't care less she knew that she had turned me on.

"I...umm...I didn't think about what I was saying," she stuttered.

I handed the MP working the gate my ID. After he checked it and waved me through, I decided it was time to be clear about my intentions.

"I'm going to be honest with you. The first night I saw you at Lenox's house I was trying to figure out a way to get you to leave with me. After we spoke for a few hours, I was trying to come up with an excuse to spend more time with you because I knew you were different. I didn't know why you were, but you were. When Lenox mentioned Jason, the door shut, and you were off limits. And not because I don't like kids. Because I knew you needed someone who could make you promises. You need a man who could offer you a future. Emily, I cannot make you any promises. I have no idea if...I need time." I paused a moment trying to choose my words carefully. "There's no denying I'm attracted to you. You are a stunning woman. Every time I'm around you I'm fighting a hard-on. Yes, that includes when you're crying in my arms. Yet, it's more than that. I feel different when I'm around you. Women don't look past what they think is good-looking, they never see me. For some inexplicable reason, I feel like you do."

Emily remained quiet, and I was worried I offended her. We pulled in front of the 707, and I parked. I still hadn't had time to fill her in completely about Liam. It would have to wait now. I pulled the keys out of the ignition and started to open my door when her soft hand wrapped around my bicep getting my attention.

"That night I met you, I remember thinking that you might very well be the sexiest man I had ever laid eyes on. When you winked at me, you did crazy things to my girly parts, and I wanted to pull you into the bathroom and have a go. Then after we talked, I couldn't bring myself to take advantage of you that way. I couldn't use you. I may not know what caused it, but I know it's there – pain lingers behind your eyes. You mask it well yet if you pay attention it is clear as day. You don't have to ever tell me what hurt you so deeply. As long as you know, I see it."

She didn't wait for me to respond. She opened her door and got out. The slamming door pulled me from my stupor. If it wasn't so fucking sad, it would be funny – this little slip of a woman didn't want to take advantage of me.

She saw me. Now I had to figure out what to do about it.

Was it possible for me to make promises?

CHAPTER NINE

Emily

Jasper had barely looked at me since my outburst in the car. He walked us into the building housing the 707 research and development team. The entrance to the building looked like any other Battalion Brigade – plain and boring with an American flag proudly displayed. The Sergeant behind the desk greeted Jasper. They exchanged a few words that I missed due to my curiosity. Now that I knew Jasper and the guys were not in charge of gear, I was being nosey and trying to look around for new clues about what they really did. As if the entryway would display mission maps and top-secret information would just be laying around on the desk. However, I couldn't help myself from searching.

"Emily?" Jasper called out to me.

He nodded his head toward the door motioning for me to follow him.

"He didn't need my ID?" I asked.

"No. But you need to wear this while we are in this building." He handed me a laminated blue badge. I flipped it over noting the word *Visitor* was missing. Without asking any questions, I slipped the lanyard around my neck and followed him down a long corridor.

Once we stopped at the door at the end of the hall, Jasper slid his security card through the reader and placed his hand on the fingerprint scanner. The lock clicked open, and he pulled the door open, allowing me to enter first.

Lenox, Connor, Levi, and Clark were all sitting around a large conference table.

"Bout time your lazy ass showed up," Levi said.

"Dude! What the hell? No clean clothes this morning?" Clark asked.

I glanced at Jasper, realizing that we never made it to his house for him to change. He was still wearing the coffee-stained tee. Once again embarrassment washed over me as I remembered this morning's mishap.

"Jason's school took longer than I thought. We

didn't have time to stop by my place." Thankfully Jasper didn't elaborate on how the stain got there.

"Hey, Emily. How are you holding up?" Lenox asked.

"Honestly? I'm not sure," I answered him.

"Fair enough. There's a lot going on. We'll get everything sorted," he tried to assure me.

There was more going on than Lenox knew. I wasn't all that confident that the situation would get sorted without my heart getting broken in the process. I had to push my sad, nonexistent love life out of my head and concentrate on getting Liam out of my life. The sooner that happened, the faster Jasper would leave. Once I wasn't in danger, he wouldn't feel compelled to hang around, and maybe I could escape with a minor fracture rather than a full-on gaping hole in my heart. Or worse, I would break down and beg him to take me to bed, making me no better than all the women who used Jasper without a thought to him as a person.

Connor was watching me from where he sat. I was afraid to look directly at him. He had an uncanny ability to read my emotions, and I didn't want him to see my inner turmoil. Clark stood and announced we were leaving and going to a place called the hangar. We exited the building out a back-door where there was an awaiting SUV. We all piled in, and Clark drove us to the far end of the base, passing through several security checkpoints before we pulled up to what looked like an old, well, hangar.

Once we made our way to the hangar and the door was closed behind us, Levi turned to Connor.

"This room's known as a *SCIF*, a compartmented information facility. Meaning that this building is reinforced with anti-ballistic material, which also provides security from anyone trying to listen. As an added precaution, there are jammers both inside the room as well as outside. There's no radio transmission in or out of this room so your cell phone will not work here when they are on. For all intents and purposes, this area is a dead zone. You may speak freely while we are here. The main building at the 707 is equipped with standard Army security protocol. It is not secure, therefore, watch what you say."

Once Levi was done with his explanation, he started turning on computers and monitors. Clark unpacked a backpack that had manila file folders and set them on a long table with no chairs. As a matter of fact, when I looked around the room, I noticed there were very little furnishings. Five workstations, one table, whiteboards on the wall, and two couches facing a large flat screen in the corner sectioned off part of the room. The other corner had a fridge and a small kitchenette. There were five lockers on the wall near the fridge. What caught my attention the most was a chain-link enclosure in the middle of the room. It looked like one of those outside dog kennels on steroids. I couldn't make out what was in the enclosure.

"We keep our gear in there," Jasper explained when he saw me staring. "It's safe to touch it now, but when the alarm's set, if you touch the cage it will shock the shit out of you. Levi has it wired at two thousand volts. That's roughly the amount of voltage of the electric chair. I'll spare you the physics lesson, but the amperes are low enough it wouldn't kill you if you touched it but could singe your eyebrows."

"Wow." That sounded pretty serious.

"Ironically, I am the one who maintains the gear. I guess you were partially correct when you thought I audited gear." Jasper laughed.

How could I've been so stupid to think that Lenox and his team sat behind a computer and audited gear?

"Let's get to it," Clark announced. "I'm really sorry to have to dig through your life, Emily, but I need you to start at the beginning and tell us every-thing you know about Liam Gains."

Bile rose up and a mixture of embarrassment and fear wrapped itself around my throat. I didn't want to talk about Liam, not in front of these men.

"Nothing leaves this room," Lenox assured me.

I trusted that none of them would say anything, but I was more concerned that Jasper would know how stupid and desperate I was after Brian died.

With a quick exhale, I told my story before I could chicken out. I told them about how I met Liam, how he was kind and generous until I started asking him how he always had so much money to spoil me and live in such a nice apartment. That's when I had to tell them how he started hitting me and how dumb I was to stay. The first time I found a stash of drugs and cash in his closet and how we fought and I tried to leave. But by that time, it was too late and he wouldn't let me. My mom had completely shut down after Brian's death and was oblivious to anything going on around her. She couldn't help me, and I had no one else. I told them the names of everyone in his crew and where I remember them living. And finally, I told them about Steven and how he saved me.

"And Liam never tried to contact you or Steven after you left?" Clark asked.

"Not me. Steven never told me if he had tried to contact him," I told him.

"Steven made it clear to Liam that if he ever tried to come near Emily again, he would be sorry. Steven had something over Liam," Connor interjected. "A gun. It was used in a robbery when they were in high school. Liam and Brian held up a liquor store, and the shop owner and his wife were killed. Steven never came forward because it would implicate his best friend, too. He thought he was protecting Brian. He deeply regretted that decision and blamed himself for Brian's death. It was shortly after the robbery that Brian started to use heavily. If Steven had turned them in, Brian most likely would be in jail for murder or accessory, but he might still be alive. I'm sorry, Emily. Steven never wanted you to know."

I vaguely remembered the liquor store being robbed. Steven and my brother were older than me. When they were graduating high school, I was still in middle school. I was stuck on Steven covering up a murder part. Is that why he looked out for me? Out of guilt, not because he was my friend? I couldn't even begin to process that my brother possibly murdered two people. That would explain his sudden drug use and why he pulled away from my mom and me. Our dad left when I was too young to even remember him. My mom blamed Brian's drug use on growing up without a father. She needed something to blame at the time.

"Where are you on the confidential informant notation?" Clark continued.

I was grateful that he was moving the conversation away from my brother.

"Detective Cummings of the Petersburg PD is the point man for Gains. Officially, Gains, out of the kindness of his heart, informed Cummings of a drug shipment being transported by a local motorcycle club. We know that's bullshit; I have feelers out trying to get the scoop on what really happened," Connor said.

"Peter Cummings?" I asked.

"Yeah, you know him?"

"Yes, Peter went to school with Brian and Liam. Peter was in and out of Liam's house frequently. They discussed patrol routes."

"So, Cummings is a hack. What a fucking disgrace to the badge," Connor snarled. He hated dirty cops. Connor was proud to have served on the force before becoming a Marshal.

"Gains and Cummings work together to try and keep Gains' runs as clean as possible, but he has him in the system as a CI in case he gets jacked up on a delivery. The cops won't touch Gains. To make it look legit, Gains snitched on an MC. Also, this clears the path for more drug sales if the competition is out of the game. Gains branches out and starts running drugs down here." Jasper pieced together as Lenox wrote on the whiteboard. "The dumb fuck Miller becomes a distributor for Gains here on base."

The door opened, and a large man walked in. "You ladies better have something good for me," his voice boomed in the large space. He came to a stop in front of Jasper. "What, is today show and tell or bring your girlfriend to work day?" The man looked at me, and I had the sudden urge to run and hide. His stare was lethal. "I thought you said that Emily Jenkins wouldn't be an issue?"

Connor started to speak but wisely stopped when Jasper put his hand up. "There's been a new development. We needed intel from her," Jasper explained.

"And you're personally taking responsibility for her?" the man asked.

"Roger, Commander."

Holy shit, this man was the Commander? No one saluted him when he walked in the door.

"You may be one of my best operatives, but so

help me God, if this goes sideways I will have your ass in a sling. You'll be in a hole so fast your hair will catch fire."

"Copy that."

After the Commander was done chewing Jasper's ass, he turned to me. "Ma'am, first let me say I'm sorry for your loss. Jenkins was a fine man, one I am proud to have served with. I assume you understand the circumstances you find yourself in are precarious at best. You are not to talk about these men to anyone – not your mother, your friends, hell, not even your priest. This unit does not exist. While I appreciate your personal sacrifice to this nation, your behind will be right next to Jasper's if you breathe a word about these men." Jasper's growl could be heard in the now silent room. "You have a problem, son?"

"Quite frankly I do, sir. The fact that you find it necessary to threaten Emily tells me that you don't trust not only my judgment but my competency. Emily has been briefed; as has Deputy O'Brien. Neither of them would be in this room now if they had not been fully vetted and it was not pertinent to the operation."

"Trust but verify," the Commander said.

"Yes, sir, I fully understand," I managed to squeak out.

"If you'd like, you can go sit on the couch. We'll come and get you if we have any more questions," Jasper whispered to me. "I'm sorry you're stuck here."

"Thanks. I'll do that."

I made my way to the couch on shaky legs, giving myself a wide clearance from the electrified cage of death. I plopped down on the worn-out sofa and wondered why in the world Jasper would put his career and freedom on the line for me. Not that it would be an issue, I'd never say anything to anyone. However, the fact remained him bringing me here meant he trusted me with his life and the lives of his team.

I wasn't sure what to make of that.

CHAPTER TEN

Jasper

I was relieved when Connor kept his mouth shut, him jumping to Emily's defense would've only made the situation worse. The Commander was a straight shooter; if he had a problem with what you were doing, he told you. I had been expecting to get my ass chewed for having Emily here. I hadn't cleared it with the Commander. I made the decision to bring her with me without anyone's prior knowledge, but I wasn't taking any chances with her safety. Also, because I was afraid she'd follow through and pack up and leave. I couldn't let that happen. There was the added benefit that she had useful intel that saved us time. The connection between Gains and Cummings would've been made; however, it would've taken us a few hours to find. A few hours we didn't have.

"What did you get on Philips?" the Commander asked, completely ignoring Connor's presence, which irked me even more. He had read Emily the riot act yet had said nothing to Connor.

"I was about to brief the team now," Levi said, "I've spent what was left of last night putting wiretaps into place. Our boy has been busy this morning. You want the good news or the bad news first?"

"Good news," I answered.

"Good news is Phillips is a chatty motherfucker. He made a call to his girlfriend."

"Phillips is married," I interjected.

"He is. Has been for almost twenty years. His girlfriend, Beverly, however, lives in town with their three-year-old daughter. His next call was to his bookie to bet on a baseball game and to see when and where the next poker game would be. The next call proved to be the most help. Phillips called a guy named Max Stevenson and said he needed to score and asked him if he had a hookup. Stevenson told him that he knew someone who could help him out. Said he'd let him know when and where as soon as he got a hold of Gains."

"The bad news?" Clark asked.

"We have a dirty, womanizing, gambling, coke head in our ranks. Who, by the way, sold information to Roman." Levi smiled.

"Asshole, you could've lead with that," Lenox grumbled, still writing on the whiteboard.

Lenox had everything mapped out like a fucked-up family tree of criminals and how everyone intersected with each other. Written at the top of the board was the one question that was burning my gut: *Did Gains know that Emily worked at the bank?*

After everything Connor had told us about Steven having the murder weapon, it was doubtful Gains would take the chance and seek out Emily. Unless he thought since Steven was dead, there was no longer a threat.

"Something's bothering me," I blurted out. "The branch manager. He had a self-inflicted gunshot. Why would the manager kill himself? Who picked that bank to rob and why?"

"If you hadn't killed two of them, we might've been able to ask," Clark shot back.

"Does anyone care I found the connection between Phillips and Roman?" Levi asked.

"Did we run a background check on the manager?" I asked.

"Christ. Yes, I did. He was meaningless," Levi

said, disappointed we were not jumping on the information about Roman. I hated loose ends, and the manager was unaccounted for.

"The manager was Miller's stepfather. Not too far of a stretch to figure it was an inside job. The report says he never even came out of his office," Connor said, reading from the file in his hand. "He and his wife were in financial ruin with the attorney's fees they were paying for Miller. They also took a second mortgage out on the house, which Emily did process."

"Not surprised, she was the only loan officer at that branch." I didn't like that Connor threw that last part in. There was no way she had any involvement.

"Easy, Rambo. I of all people know that Emily's clean. Simply stating the facts. His wife had also filed for divorce, citing infidelity." He finished and put the file back on the table.

"Levi, whatcha got?" I asked.

"Those weekly deposits came from an account in the Caymans. It was another one of Roman's fronts. A business account that had deposits made into it from Roman's account we tracked to Nova Scotia. The same account he used to donate money to Lily's Charity."

The vein in the side of Lenox's neck looked like

it was ready to explode. I couldn't blame him. Roman had found Lily and stalked her. After Lenox had tried to hide her away, he even went as far as to fake his own death to keep her safe. Lenox gave up twelve years with the woman he loved, and Roman had almost killed her.

"How do we handle this, Commander?" Clark asked.

This was going to get tricky. We were on American soil. There were rules here, rules we did not play by when we were in theatre.

"Motherfucker, clusterfuck of shit," the Commander muttered. "Goddamn, what's happening to this base? Are there any soldiers left who still believe in loyalty, morality, and service? All I see are a bunch of weak-minded dopers who steal and sell-out their country. Has Phillips been in contact with anyone else about the information he has access to?"

"Negative," Levi answered.

"Sit on his ass and listen. Before we take him out, I want to know for sure."

"Copy that." Levi turned and started typing on his laptop.

"And Gains?" I asked.

"Find him, and bring him to the shed. Let's find

out what he knows before we turn him over." The Commander pinned me with his stare. "I don't suppose if I told you not to do anything stupid you'd listen?"

"No, sir. I will do whatever I have to, to protect Emily and Jason. I will make sure there's no blow-back on the team."

"Christ Almighty! And if you get caught? You're willing to throw your career away? Your team?" he pressed.

I loved my job, and my teammates were brothers to me. I didn't love Emily, and I was still trying to reconcile if there was even a chance for us, but my answer came quick. It was a no-brainer, I'd give it up if it meant Emily and Jason were safe.

"Yes," I answered him.

The Commander took a minute to mull over my answer. When he spoke again, he was looking directly at Connor. "You can leave now if you feel so compelled, Mr. U.S. Marshal. I mean no disrespect by that. You vowed to uphold the law. This next conversation might not be so lawful."

"I'm straight," Connor said.

"If she means that much to you, I'll have your back if the need were to arise. But Sweet Jesus, try not to kill him. I can pull a lot of strings, but if there are witnesses, it's gonna be a cluster. I just got you off the hook for the last two bodies. A murder charge will be difficult."

"Copy that."

"Alright, ladies. There's work to do, get to it."

The Commander didn't wait for us to say our goodbyes before he was out the door.

"We'll wait and see if Phillips makes contact with Gains. Hopefully, they give us a time and place for the drop. We'll grab Gains from there," Clark said.

I was torn between going with my team to pick up Gains and staying with Emily and Jason. I'm sure Connor would stay with them if I asked, but I didn't trust anyone with her safety. Not even Connor.

"I'll take Emily to go run her errands and pick up Jason from school. Somewhere in there, I have to stop by my place to shower and change clothes," I told the guys.

"You staying with her?" Lenox asked.

"Abso-fuckin-lutely."

"Lily would love to see her. She doesn't know about this newest threat, but she's worried because Emily hasn't been around much since the robbery."

I already knew that. When I wasn't at work, I

had been following Emily. She had only stopped by Lenox's house twice in the last month.

"As soon as we have a lock on Gains, I'll bring her over. I don't want to bring Gains to your doorstep."

"Roger," he agreed.

Levi, Clark, and Lenox went about getting to work, and I was ignoring Connor's death stare by scanning the whiteboard. However, after a solid two minutes of feeling his eyes trying to bore holes in my head, I couldn't tune it out anymore. When I fully turned toward him, his brows were pinched together, and he looked pissed. I wanted to question him again about his relationship with Emily. If I didn't know any better, I'd think he was jealous.

"Would you like to step outside to do this so Emily doesn't hear?" I asked.

"You gonna get loud?" he asked.

"It depends on what you have to say. Because I gotta tell you, with everything going on, my patience is worn thin. I'm still pissed you looked into me. Even though I get it, it doesn't make me happy. And at the moment I'm more concerned with Emily and Jason than what you think of me, or if I'll *man up*."

"I think you proved today that you are more than capable of manning up. I was gonna say thank you for taking Emily's back with your Commander. And see if there was anything I can help you with."

"Yeah, there is. How well do you know Emily's mom?" I asked.

"Well."

"Is she a rational woman?"

I needed to know if I was walking into a land-mine with the mom.

"Hell no. That woman will lose her shit if she thinks Emily's in trouble, and not in a normal Mama Bear way. She will come apart and have a nervous breakdown, meaning that Emily will have to take care of her."

That was the last thing we needed. I didn't want Emily stressed out over her mom. I needed her mind on her surroundings and staying vigilant about safety.

"I need you to have my back on a few things," I told him.

"Whatever you need."

"First, I'm sending Emily's mom on a trip to California. I need her someplace safe and away from Emily. We need a good excuse, and the trip should come from you. Tell me what you come up with, and I'll book her a ticket, but it needs to be today. The other thing I need is if Emily tells you she's moving away, you discourage her. I've told her twice now she's not moving, but she says she wants to run. I need them here. I cannot protect them if I have to chase her ass down."

"Did you just hear what you said?" he asked.

What the hell was he talking about? "Send Emily's mom to California. Don't let her move or I can't watch out for her?" I repeated.

"You said *them*. Tell her, Jasper. And don't worry about Betsy. I'll go over there now and tell her she's going on vacation. I'll explain I bought a ticket to go but have to work and I don't want it going to waste. She'll jump on it. As far as them leaving, over my dead body is she going anywhere."

"Pushy prick," I grumbled, and Connor laughed. "I appreciate your concern, but it's not your fucking business."

"She's my business. Always will be. I'm telling you this man to man, pull your head out of your ass and claim that woman before you lose her completely. If I know Emily at all, she's over there thinking of all the reasons she needs to push you away. The newest addition to the list is you fucking up your job because of her."

I looked at Emily, and sure enough, she was

curled into herself on the couch worrying her bottom lip, deep in thought.

Hell no! That wasn't going to do.

"Soon," I told him.

I needed to talk to Clark. He was always the voice of reason on the team. I knew what Lenox and Levi would say. But Clark, he was a man with his own secrets; he'd know what was going on in my head.

"I'm going to see Betsy. I'll text you when it's done."

"Thanks."

Connor said his goodbyes to the guys and made his way over to Emily. I caught Clark's attention and gestured for him to follow me outside. The door was barely closing when Clark came through it, followed by Lenox and Levi.

"Don't roll your eyes." Clark laughed. "I thought you could tell us all at once. Save you the hassle of three individual conversations."

Now that I had them all in front of me, I wasn't sure what it was I wanted to ask Clark about.

"What's stopping you?" Lenox asked.

"She has a kid."

"And?" Levi asked.

"And? And?" Fuck me, I was stuttering. I couldn't put into words how I felt.

"And you don't think you can be a dad, or more to the point, you should ever be a dad again because of Alesha." Clark helpfully finished what I was trying to say.

"Something like that, yes."

"You still feel responsible for Alesha being stillborn."

"I am responsible," I told him.

"I get it. Fuck do I ever get it, the weight of guilt is crippling." Clark's eyes clouded over like he remembered something painful. "It's time to stop being a dumbass. You deserve to be happy. You need to talk to her."

"I can't. What if she doesn't trust me to take care of her and Jason when I tell her I couldn't even keep my daughter safe?"

"I don't mean to sound like an insensitive dick here, but you couldn't protect Alesha. What happened was a tragic accident."

"I'm gonna give you a taste of your own medicine. You have twenty-four hours to figure your shit out. If you don't, then I'm stepping in and taking over. You kept not only Lily away from me, but the fact that she was carrying my baby a secret for my own good so I could get my head on straight. Consider this me returning the favor. You need your head in the game, and you can't do that while your emotions are all over the place. Priority one is keeping her safe, you getting a piece of ass isn't even on my radar," Lenox said.

I was dangerously close to losing my temper. "Don't you ever call Emily a piece of ass. Over my dead fucking body you'll take them away from me."

I stomped to the door trying to tamp down my anger. I loved Lenox like a brother, but if he thought I was going to step aside and let him take care of Emily and Jason, he was dead wrong.

"Good talk." Clark laughed.

"You assholes coming?" I asked as I held open the door.

"You make a decision?" Lenox asked.

"Seems so."

Now I had to find a way to explain to Emily that my daughter died because I was a low-life, deadbeat father who denied his own child.

CHAPTER ELEVEN

Emily

"Hey."

I was so lost in thought I hadn't heard Connor walk up. It was hard to wrap my mind around what Steven had done to protect Brian, what Liam and Brian had done in the first place. They were murderers. Jason's biological father was a drug dealing murderer! How could I have been so stupid? And now Jasper knew.

"Hey. Sorry to drag you into all of this," I said.

"Stop, Emily. You didn't drag me into anything. I need to fill you in on a few things before I go."

"Okay." I stopped fiddling with the hem on my T-shirt and gave him my full attention.

"I'm sorry we never told you about the liquor

store." Connor was gracious enough not to say anything further.

"Is that why Steven helped me? Because he felt guilty about Brian?" I asked. That was the part that was really bothering me, the thought that I was more of an inconvenience to him.

"No. Steven did what he did because you were like a sister to him. He loved you. Truthfully, once I understood the situation, I would've been disappointed in him if he had not." Connor grabbed my hand and held onto it. "I don't think Liam's here for Jason. I don't even think he knows. Remember when you first moved in with Steven and you were organizing all the stuff you brought with you? There was an address book, and you threw it away?"

I thought back to when I first got to Georgia. My life was in complete shambles. I only brought a suitcase with my clothes and a few trash bags full of stuff I had at Liam's place. I was more or less living there at the time. However, most of my belongings were still at my mom's.

"Vaguely. I remember I accidentally took some of Liam's stuff and wanted to get rid of it. There was an address book I thought it was mine, so I grabbed it. But there was nothing in it." Why was an old address book from over six years ago important? "Why else would Liam be here if not for Jason?"

"I think he wants the book back," he explained.

"Why? It was basically empty except for a few numbers, but no names. Not to mention, he heard Jason in the house and asked for him by name."

"I don't think they are *just numbers*. And a simple search of your name and he'd easily find Jason's name. You haven't exactly been hiding out all these years. You have a Facebook page with photos of Jason. Thankfully, the kid's a spitting image of you and looks nothing like Liam."

Facebook! Damn social media! He was right, I hadn't been careful. There are pictures of us all over the place. It's not like I changed my name or anything, and he knew Steven, so after we got married he could've found us at any time.

"Why wait so long? He could've looked for us at any time."

"Steven. He would never have come near you because he knew Steven had the gun."

Yes, the gun. I had forgotten about that part.

"Where's it now?" I asked.

"In my safe in an evidence bag along with the book."

My eyes felt like they were going to bug out of

my head. "WHAT?" I lowered my voice to a whisper. "You're a Marshal, you're obstructing, or whatever it's called. You can't have that, you can go to jail."

"Do you honestly think I wouldn't do whatever it took to keep you and Jason safe? Hell, Steven, too. It was better to be locked up in my safe, than laying around your house."

"I have to move, Connor. I can't keep asking all of you to put your asses on the line. First you and Steven, now Jasper. You heard the Commander. He was red-hot pissed I was here. Jasper could lose his job and go to prison. Military prison. This isn't right. Give Liam the book, and Jason and I will leave. I'll be smart this time and change our names. Hell, you put people in witness protection all the time, you can teach me what to do. I'll listen, I promise."

This had to end. Good men were putting their livelihood and freedom on the line. For what? A stupid decision I made and a book.

"Jasper knows what he's doing. He did put his ass on the line, more than you realize. So I want you to listen to me. You are not going anywhere. He can protect you here. We all can. This is bigger than a book and Jason. Liam Gains is more dangerous now than he was when you met him. He has to be stopped. Our best bet is to do that now, here in Georgia. I also wanted to tell you in the best interest of your sanity, Jasper will be sending your mom on an all-expenses-paid trip to California. I'm going over there now to tell her the good news. When she calls you to tell you about it, be excited for her. She'll think the trip is from me, a vacation I can't take because of work."

"No. Absolutely not is Jasper paying for that. Just no. This has to end. Why, why is he doing all of this? It's too much, Connor." I couldn't stop the tears from welling in my eyes. "He knows all about my past, he must think I'm total trash now. My brother, my ex, my shitty choices."

"I do not think you're trash," Jasper thundered.

I didn't say anything. Instead, I pretended to be an ostrich and closed my eyes. If I couldn't see him, I didn't have to acknowledge he had heard what I said.

"I'm gonna go talk to your mom." Connor tugged me up with him and pulled me in for a hug. "He's doing this for you whether you want him to or not. He obviously cares about you. You need to hear him out," Connor whispered into my ear.

With a kiss on my cheek, he left me standing with one pissed off looking man. I wanted to run after Connor and beg him to take me with him.

Dealing with my mom had to be better than facing Jasper.

"You ready?" he asked.

I opted for a nonverbal answer and simply nodded.

I followed behind Jasper like a lost puppy unsure of what the plan was, yet too scared to ask.

"I'll be at Emily's waiting for your call," he told the guys.

"Copy that."

We got to the front door when suddenly he changed directions and went back to a desk, opening the drawer grabbing a cell phone. "Call me on comm two, in case Jason wants to play a game on my phone again."

Jason? He was thinking about Jason?

He drove us back to the 707 building, and I wondered how the others would get back. My question died in my throat when he parked, and I saw the Commander standing outside the building smoking a cigar.

"Everyone straight?" the Commander asked when we approached.

"Roger," Jasper answered.

The Commander blew out a large plume of smoke and pinned me with his stare. "You listen to

Jasper, follow his instructions to the T. He'll get you through this shit storm. It won't take long."

"Yes, sir."

"Please, call me Ben," the Commander offered, his tone softening.

"Thank you, Ben. I'm sorry for all the trouble I've caused."

"No trouble, as long as you remember the code by which these men live and die by. You now hold secrets that could very easily get one of these men killed. I trust you understand the severity of that responsibility."

"I understand," I assured him.

"Hey Jasper, you think you can show up for work tomorrow not looking like you just rolled out of bed from a week long bender?" Ben asked.

"Depends on how tonight goes," Jasper responded.

Ben choked on the cigar smoke and shook his head.

The Commander offered me a smile and motioned me to follow Jasper who had already opened the door to the building. Checking out of the 707 was done much the same way as when I entered. Only this time I didn't search the room for super cool commando secrets. I now knew where those were kept.

Jasper beeped the locks and opened my door. Before I could get in the car he caged me in. His face, and therefore full, perfect lips, were only inches from mine. Was he going to kiss me? It sure felt like he was going to.

"We need to talk." His breath on my face awoke a desire I hadn't felt in a long time, if ever. "I'm taking you back to my house before this goes any farther – there are things you need to know. It's only fair you have all the facts before you decide if you want to proceed."

I couldn't concentrate on his words when I was so enthralled with the way his lips moved as he spoke. I nodded my head though I wasn't sure what I was agreeing to.

"Em, I'm going to kiss you now. Tell me to stop if you don't want that."

Was he crazy? Tell him to stop, I could no more tell him to stop than I could fly.

His face inched closer to mine at an agonizingly slow pace. When his lips finally met mine, I was expecting him to – well, I wasn't sure what I was expecting, but it wasn't the soft brush of his lips against mine.

Jasper took his time in a gentle exploration of my lips before he slowly licked the seam causing me to open for him. With the first stroke of his tongue against mine, he owned me. My eyes rolled into the back of my head, and my girly part clenched.

This man was going to ruin me.

CHAPTER TWELVE

Jasper

After we cleared the guard gate leaving the base, I sped down the highway breaking every posted speed limit on the way to my house. Five miles had never felt so long. I literally had been stunned into silence. Never had a kiss felt so right. Maybe it should have scared the shit out of me that she could tie me up with one kiss, but instead, I was excited. I don't think I'd ever been this eager to get to know a woman, explore her, learn her mind and body. I was even excited about the possibility of a future.

Everything hinged on the talk.

What if she wanted to walk away after I told her? Could I? Would I step aside and let her go and find someone who deserved her loyalty and affection?

Before I could come up with a plan to stop her if she tried to bolt, we pulled into my driveway.

I owned a modest three-bedroom in a well-established neighborhood. My neighbors were polite and kept to themselves. It was nice and quiet, exactly what I needed when I actually got to spend time there. Which wasn't very often. The team didn't have regular deployment rotations; we were sent out when a situation needed to be handled. It didn't matter if it was Christmas or if we had only gotten back twenty-four hours before. When the Commander called, we left.

I reached across the center console and steadied Emily's bouncing knee.

"Nervous?" I asked.

"A little."

"Me, too," I admitted. "I want you to understand I brought you here so we could talk without Jason around. Nothing else. That and I need a change of clothes."

"Okay."

We walked through the door, and for the first time I was a little embarrassed about the décor, or lack thereof. My house was cold and sterile with two recliners positioned in front of a sixty-inch flat screen mounted on the wall above the fireplace. It was dull and lifeless compared to her well-lived-in home. She had pictures on the wall, and a soft and comfortable couch. A real home that a family lived in. I had a house, yet nothing about it felt like a home.

"I'm sorry there isn't much here. I'd offer you something to eat, but there's nothing in the fridge either." Over the last month, I hadn't even spent the night here – I spent every night in my car outside of her house. "I'm gonna go shower real quick, make yourself at home."

"Mind if I get a glass of water?" she asked.

"Help yourself to anything you can find."

I made my way down the hall into the master bedroom, grabbed some clean clothes, and rushed through a shower. The water hadn't even completely heated before I was done and getting out. Not bothering to shave which I needed to do badly. When the team was stateside, we still had to adhere to Army grooming regulations. Even if I didn't have to wear my uniform to work daily, I still had to be clean shaven. I toweled off and threw on my clothes, eager to get back to Emily.

"That was fast." She laughed when I entered the living room to find her with her shoes off curled up in one of the recliners. "Did you learn that at basic?

Seems all you Army men can shower in two point five seconds."

"Learned that having to clean up with bullets flying around you. The less time you spend with your tac vest off and your rifle in your hand the better your chance of survival."

Emily's face paled, and I wanted to kick my own ass for saying something so stupid to her. Steven died in combat. She didn't need to be reminded of the dangers of my job nor how her husband died.

"Sorry."

"Don't be, I'm fine."

I checked my watch hoping we had more time than we did. Jason would be out of school soon.

It was time.

"I have to tell you something." I sat in the other recliner and leaned forward placing my elbows on my knees, for no other reason than to stop them from shaking. I was a pussy; I could fight on the battlefield without giving my personal safety a thought, yet I couldn't talk about my daughter. "I've only ever told the guys about this, and even they don't know the whole story. Can you, um, do me a favor and just let me tell the story without any questions?"

"You don't have to do this, Jasper. I don't want

you to talk about something that obviously hurts you."

For a split second, I thought about taking the easy out she had given me and not telling her. But I couldn't. Before we moved on she had to know a few things about me, it was only fair.

"I have to."

"Okay. I won't say a word," she murmured and settled back in the recliner.

"When I was in high school, I dated a girl Liz. When we graduated, we went our separate ways. It was mutual and ended well. She went to college in Washington State and stayed there after she graduated. Over the years, if we were both back in Montana at the same time, we'd hook up. It was comfortable and it was easy, for both of us. We both understood what it was. My, um," I had to stop and take a breath. "My Granddad passed away, and she flew to Montana to go to the funeral. We spent a few days together, and just like all the other times, our time ended on a happy note, and we went back to our lives. Two months later, she called to tell me she was pregnant.

"I panicked. I asked her if she was sure the baby was mine. I don't know why. She'd never lied to me, misled me, or given me any reason not to trust her a hundred percent. Even after she promised that it couldn't have been anyone else's, I continued to question how it was possible. We got into the biggest fight we had ever had. We both said some pretty shitty things to each other. She hung up on me, and I never called her back."

I winced, remembering all the fucked-up things we had both said. Eight years of history rehashed and exaggerated because we were both upset.

"I didn't call back for six months. When I did, Liz's sister answered the phone and told me to go to hell and never call again. I called a few more times with no answer. Another month went by, and I decided to track her down. What I found instead of a current address was an obituary, for her and my daughter. That's how I found out that they had died. Because I was a dick, they were both gone. I was such a fucking coward I couldn't bring myself to face her family, so I hacked into her medical records. Liz was thirty weeks pregnant when she went to the hospital because she hadn't felt the baby move. There were no fetal heart tones when she arrived and the doctor induced labor."

I hadn't realized that Emily had moved until she sat at my feet pushing my elbow out of the way so she could lay her head on my knee. Just her closeness seemed to calm my racing heart some. I gathered her hair off her face and ran my hand over the back of her head to smooth it.

"The doctor induced labor and Liz died giving birth to my daughter. Alesha's cause of death was listed as an umbilical cord accident." I continued to stroke Emily's hair, needing the connection. "The last words I ever heard the mother of my child say to me were, *I've never been so disappointed in you.* Then she hung up."

"I'm so sorry," Emily whispered, her voice full of emotion.

"I don't deserve your tears, Emily. I did this to them. I'm an asshole. I turned my back on the mother of my child. But worse than that, I let one of my closest friends down. I abandoned her when she needed me the most. What kind of man does that make me?"

There it was, the part that weighed heavily on my conscience. I let Liz down in the worst way possible. When she was scared and lost, I ran. I should've been there for her, for our child. What must she have gone through having to deliver Alesha knowing she was already gone. I should've been there. Instead, I was a weak, spineless bastard who let her die alone and devastated.

"You didn't do anything to them. What happened to Alesha and Liz was a horrible series of tragic events. Even if you had been there, you couldn't have stopped it." Emily's words of consolation fell flat. There was nothing she could say that would absolve me of the guilt I felt.

"I don't want to hurt you, Emily, or Jason. That's why once I found out that you had a child I didn't go after you. I'm fucked up. I don't know if I can make you promises about the future. Hell, I don't even deserve to be around Jason. My lack of care for my own child proves that."

Damn, admitting my shortcomings hurt like a bitch. Never had I laid myself bare in front of a woman the way I had with Emily. It had nothing to do with Lenox's threat or Connor's urging. There was something about Emily that made me want to open up and let her see me, my faults and scars included.

I wanted this woman in the worst kind of way. Emily was the only one who could soothe the ache in my chest – she was the cure. She was my only hope of salvation.

She now had the power to destroy me.

CHAPTER THIRTEEN

Emily

I knew the man had demons, some sort of pain that embedded itself into his bones. If you took the time to look at him, you could see it was always present. However, I never would've guessed it was the death of his child and the woman carrying his baby. With him being in the military, naturally I thought it had to do with the loss of someone in battle. I couldn't imagine what they had all gone through. I knew how much I loved my son, and I didn't think I'd be able to move on if something happened to him.

I now understood his unease around Jason and baby Carter, Lily and Lenox's son. It wasn't that he didn't like kids, he was uncomfortable around them.

A reminder of what he had lost. And here he was trying to sort my shit out, putting himself in constant close proximity to Jason. Another reason it might be better for me to leave. Only now, I didn't want to run. My thoughts and emotions were all over the place. I had to make a decision here and now. This was not me. I wasn't wishy-washy and indecisive. I was strong. Stay and fight, or leave and give up on Jasper. Connor would be mad; however, he'd get over it. Jasper would never forgive me. I would be throwing away any chance I had with him. Though he said it himself, he didn't know if he was capable of being with me. Jason. Could I stay and keep Jason safe?

Jasper's leg was still shaking under my cheek. My heart broke for him. He was so strong, he put on a good front pretending to always be happy. Joking and flirting to hide his pain. And everyone around him let him get away with it.

"I don't think you'd hurt me or Jason. I think that everything that happened with you and Liz was circumstantial. I can't pretend to know what was going through your head when she told you she was pregnant, but I do know that had Alesha lived, you would've been there for them. You would've taken care of them and been a good father. I'm sure you were both taken by surprise and emotional, and you both said things to each other that neither of you meant. We tend to lash out at those who are closest to us, the ones we know love us because we know we are safe with them. It doesn't make it right, it's just true."

Jasper's knee started to bounce a little harder, and I wrapped my arms around his leg to hold it still.

"You know what I was doing while Liz was alone carrying our baby?"

"I don't," I answered. "But I can imagine."

Somehow, I didn't think I wanted to hear what Jasper was doing all those months.

"I was out picking up women, not giving two shits about my responsibilities to Liz."

My stomach twisted thinking about Jasper blowing through most of the women in the county, hell, most likely the state. Not out of disgust but jealousy. I was jealous he'd been with so many women.

"I want to proceed," I told him.

"Proceed?" he asked.

I had made my decision. With a fire in my belly and new-found confidence I explained, "Earlier, you said you wanted me to have all the facts before we took things any further. We talked. Now I'm telling you I want to proceed. There are no guarantees in life, no promises can be made about the future. Neither of us knows if this will work out, but I want to see where it goes. The only promise I need from you is that you will treat Jason with kindness and not let him get hurt if things don't work out. I'm not asking you to play daddy to my son, but I am asking you to treat him with respect. I'm a big girl and can handle my own heart, but he's only six."

Jasper was silent for so long I was worried he was trying to find a way to let me down easy. The promise I needed regarding Jason was a hard line for me. Either he promised, or he didn't. If he didn't, I was prepared to walk away with a broken heart. Better to do it now than later on. Jason had to come first.

"I promise," Jasper finally said, and relief washed over me.

I didn't know what this meant for us, but I wanted to jump up and dance I was so excited.

"We need to talk about something else." Jasper's tone brought me back to reality, all thoughts of dancing evaporated.

"About?" I prompted.

"We hope to have a lock on Liam by tonight. If not, I will continue to stay out in the Camaro and watch your house. We need to be vigilant about security; I had my security guy update your alarm system. Jason's school needs to stay alert, which means I will have another talk with them. Also, when you are not with me, I need you to stay at home with the alarm on. I can drive you anywhere you need to be and Jason to and from school. I'm not asking this of you to be a controlling dick, I need this, Em. I need to know you and Jason are safe."

I thought about his requests, and while I was more than a little ticked off he had spent more money on me, especially after the God knew how much on the trip for my mom, I wouldn't fight with him about this. Partly because Jason's safety was most important to me, and the other reason, he said he needed this from me. For his peace of mind, I would do as he asked.

"On one condition," I said. "You don't sleep in your car. That makes me feel...bad. You can sleep in the guest room or the couch." It was on the tip of my tongue to say, *or my bed preferably*. However, at this juncture that might be a tad too forward. Though I wouldn't mind it. Actually I really, really wanted him in my bed. Thoughts of us naked and him using that wicked tongue of his on all the sensitive areas of my body had me damn near panting with need.

"What about Jason? How will you explain me

staying with you?" he asked.

The man was worried about whether or not he deserved to be around Jason when he continuously proved he was putting Jason's safety and needs first. *Jason might want to play on his cell phone. Jason's school needed to be kept up to date. What will Jason think?* He couldn't see past his guilt. That was going to have to change.

"I'll tell him...your house is being fumigated." I smiled at the easy solution.

"As long as you're both comfortable with it, I'll take the couch," he agreed.

"Great. Pack a bag and let's go pick up Jason." I scooched out from between his legs and stood up.

"Damn, you're bossy, woman." Jasper laughed.

"You have no idea." I winked.

Jasper was on his feet invading my space, with his hands loosely fisting my hair before I could take my next breath.

"Is that so?" His lips were once again close, so damn close I wanted to remove the space but was enjoying his playfulness too much to stop it.

"You think you can handle my bossy side?" I whispered trying not to inch forward.

"The question is can you handle me?"

Jasper jerked his hips forward, pressing his thick

hard-on against my belly.

"I'm not sure, but it will be damn fun trying to find out."

This time it was me who closed the distance and kissed him. I didn't take it slow like he had. Instead, I pushed my way in and took everything I needed from him. Our tongues tangled, his grip on my hair tightened, and I rubbed myself harder against his erection. He broke the kiss, but not the connection.

"Em, sweetheart, I'm gonna come in my pants if we don't stop. Your sexy little body rubbing over me is too much." My desire ratcheted up tenfold with his words and my confidence grew. "I'm serious. We have to go, and this is not how I want to get off the first time I'm with you."

He might not want the first time to be like this, but I was all for the both of us finding some relief. Jasper had awoken something in me that had laid dormant for a very long time. Not that I would ever admit this to anyone, ever, but I hadn't even mastur-bated in all these years. I had been completely celi-bate, self-love included.

He gently kissed the corner of my mouth and pulled away. I looked down as he adjusted himself in his pants. I would've gladly helped him had he asked.

"I'm gonna grab a few things. I think it's best if we hurry and leave. I only have so much control and the way you're looking down at my dick has me ready to snap."

My insides were doing somersaults at the thought of Jasper being as turned on as I was.

WE PICKED up Jason from school and made the stops I needed before we headed back to my house. Along the way, my mom had called to tell me what a doll Connor was and how he had transferred his ticket to California in her name. He had even changed the hotel reservation to a beach resort in San Diego. She prattled on and on about what a shame it was that Connor had to work but she'd always wanted to go to California. Connor had apparently also included some day excursions in her once-in-a-lifetime vacation. I was going to kill both of them. Connor and Jasper. Connor was having a grand old-time spending Jasper's money. Jasper hadn't batted an eyelash at the cost of the trip.

I didn't know what Jasper's financial situation was. However, I knew mine. It was going to take me forever to pay him back for this or I'd have to pull money out of savings. I tried not to touch that money. Steven's death benefits were supposed to be off-limits. I didn't feel right spending that money on frivolous things like sending my mom to California just so she'd be out of my hair. Well, I guess that wasn't entirely the case. It was more for her safety, I supposed. Thankfully, in my mom's excitement she hadn't asked how I was or how my job search was going.

On our way to the grocery store, I asked the guys what they wanted for dinner. Jason asked for pizza, his go-to dinner. Jasper agreed before I could tell him no. Jasper said he wanted me to relax, so either he cooked or we ordered out. I didn't want him to cook more than I didn't want pizza. The three of us walked around the store together. I was in the produce section going over my shopping list on my phone when I heard Jason ask Jasper what fumigation was.

I had told Jason that Jasper would be staying with us for a few days. He responded as I had expected, and didn't care when I asked him if he was okay with the plan.

"Sometimes when you have bugs in your house, you have to hire a fumigator to come in and kill all the bugs. The fumes are poisonous, and you can't breathe them or you'll get sick," Jasper explained.

"Bugs? What kind of bugs?" Jason questioned.

I pretended not to hear their conversation, interested in how Jasper was going to answer.

"Ants. Lots and lots of ants."

I couldn't help the laugh that broke free trying to imagine Jasper's spotless house having a single ant, let alone an infestation.

"Sometimes Mommy forgets to take out the trash and there are ants in our house. Do we need to have the poison, too?" Jason asked.

"No, bud, I'm sure your house is fine." Jasper laughed.

I couldn't believe Jason had thrown me under the bus and told Jasper we had ants. Sheesh, it's not like I forgot all the time, just sometimes...

AFTER THE DAY I'd had, I was happy to be home relaxing on my couch with a belly full of pizza — even if it wasn't my favorite — watching Jasper explain some video game on his phone to Jason. I was doing a good job keeping myself in check and not letting my mind drift to how much I wanted a family.

Not that I didn't have one now, but a family with a husband and wife and kids.

Maybe one day.

"Jason, it's time for bed," I announced.

"Mommm," he whined.

"I already gave you five more minutes. Please make sure your backpack's by the door, with your homework in it, and go brush your teeth. I'll be back to tuck you in when you're done."

"Okay. Thanks, for letting me play on your phone again, Jasper."

"Anytime, bud."

Jason handed Jasper back his phone and went about completing the task of finding his homework.

"Sorry if he ran down your battery again," I apologized.

"It's not a problem. That's why I grabbed a work phone."

Jasper had been checking his work phone all night, texting and leaving the room to take calls. I was waiting until after Jason went to bed before I asked if there were any updates on Liam.

"How long before Jason's asleep?" Jasper asked.

"He's usually out pretty fast, why?"

My girly parts started tingling again at the thought he wanted alone time with me.

"I'm gonna do a quick walk around the house and show you how to use your new alarm. After that, I want to fill you in on what's going on."

"Oh."

That was...a total let down. Though I did want an update. My idea of alone time seemed more fun than alarm instruction.

He stood when I did and blocked my path not allowing me to pass. "Disappointed?" he whispered, careful not to get too close to me in case Jason came back.

"Extremely," I answered.

"You're gonna be the death of me woman," he groaned. "Is Jason a sound sleeper?" he asked.

"Yes."

"Good because after alarm 101, I'm gonna make you scream," he vowed.

The tingling started again, and suddenly alarm one oh one didn't sound so bad.

"I can be quiet," I told him.

"Em, if you're quiet I'm doing something wrong."

"Mommm. I'm ready," Jason yelled from his bedroom.

Neither of us moved, both of us smiling. His blue eyes danced with mischief, and for the first time since I had met him, some of the shadows were gone.

CHAPTER FOURTEEN

Jasper

I checked the perimeter and walked Emily through the new alarm system. It was straightforward and much like her old one. She was so fucking cute chewing on her bottom lip in concentration. I wondered if she was really paying attention or if it was the promise of me making her scream had her daydreaming. Once the alarm was set, I told her to go get in bed and I'd be back there shortly.

"It's early," she complained.

"It's almost nine-thirty and the lights are out in the living room by ten," I reminded her.

"How do... ah, the stalking," she smiled.

"The protecting," I corrected.

Even though her tone was joking, the way she

said it made me sound like I was some perv sitting outside her house waiting to peek in on her. Not that the thought hadn't crossed my mind a time or two.

"Stalking, protecting. Eh, same difference."

She turned, and my eyes landed on her ass as she strutted back to her room. I didn't know if the sexy sway of hips was for my benefit or if that was her normal stride. I hadn't had the pleasure of watching her walk away enough to know for sure.

I checked the doors and windows and turned off the lights. After making sure everything was secured, I stood outside of her door giving myself a mental pep talk, or more honestly, I gave my dick a stern talking to.

I tapped on the door and waited for Emily to answer.

She opened the door, and I had to force myself to stand still. She had taken her long hair down and brushed it silky straight. I was a sucker for long hair. Some men like tits or ass, I liked all different shapes and sizes. Others liked a woman's smile or eyes. My number one turn on was long hair, and she had it in spades. Her pretty face was free from the minimal makeup she wore making her look younger than twenty-six. When her wide smile greeted me, I couldn't get over how gorgeous she was. She stepped aside to allow me to enter, and I had to remind my dick tonight wasn't about him.

Maybe this wasn't a good idea. I had to talk to her, and being in a room with a bed was not going to make that easy.

"You okay?" she asked.

Was I okay? Hell no. I wanted to rip her clothes off and do any number of very filthy things to her. The situation was actually comical. Me, the man that had spent years taking nameless, faceless women home, had no idea what to do. I knew what I wanted to do, but it was too soon for that.

I racked my mind for something to say, something to break the awkwardness of the moment, but I was coming up blank.

"Listen, Jasper. If you've changed your mind, I understand. No hard..." Emily started to say.

"No." Changed my mind? Shit, she had the wrong idea. "I've never done this before. I'm kinda lost here," I admitted.

"Never done...what?" she asked.

Shit, now I was making myself look like a fucking idiot.

"Let's sit down, and I'll explain."

Emily climbed on the bed and crawled to the

middle and crossed her legs Indian style. So damn cute.

"I haven't changed my mind. I've just never done this with a woman."

"Done what, Jasper? I'm not being obtuse. I just don't understand."

No, I guess she wouldn't understand because I wasn't making sense. And in order to explain, I was going to make myself sound like a douchebag.

"I've never talked about personal stuff with a woman like I have with you. Or sat on her living room floor watching Discovery channel while eating pizza. There haven't been feelings tied together with my attraction. Not since Liz. And even then, it was free and easy, a deep friendship, not a love connection. With everyone else, we fuck, I leave. End of story." She winced at my crass explanation, but that was the truth. "Other women never got any other part of me. No lingering kisses because I had to know what she tasted like. No comforting and hugging. This is different for me. There are feelings involved, and I don't want to screw it up."

"Then don't run out the door when we're done and we'll be fine," she joked.

"That's the thing. As badly as I want to jump in that bed with you and take you now, I'm not going to.

I want to do this slow. Learn you, and not just your body." I pulled my holster off my hip and set it on the nightstand and climbed on the bed, pushing her flat on her back. She struggled to get her legs uncrossed and around my hips when I settled over her. "I want to know all your secrets, your deepest desires. I want you to need me." She hooked her legs around my hips and dug her heels into my ass. "Once I'm so deep under your skin you can't find where you end and I begin, then we'll know it's time. Until then, I'm gonna enjoy every last second getting to know this body of yours." I stopped to breathe in the flowery smell on her neck, placing a few kisses there on my way to her mouth. Emily moaned and arched her back. "Oh yeah, this is gonna be so much fun."

Our lips met and our tongues tangled in an erotic dance that had my dick straining to break through the zipper of my jeans. Her lips were pillowy soft, and her tongue like velvet. She kissed me like a woman who knew what she wanted. She wasn't shy or timid; she sucked my tongue into her mouth and visions of her doing the same thing to my dick played in my mind.

She protested when I broke the kiss, lifting her head trying to keep the connection.

"My plan was to talk first, but I don't think either

of us will be able to concentrate. I want you to stop me if anything I'm doing gets to be too much or too far."

She nodded her head.

I didn't wait for her verbal consent before I pulled her T-shirt over her head and didn't waste any time unsnapping the front clasp of her bra. Full tits spilled out of the cups, and all thoughts of going slow flew out the window. I lowered my head, and my lips latched onto her nipple, sucking it fully into my mouth. There was no long drawn out sexy build up when I pushed my hand inside of her shorts and panties. Both of her hands went to my head and held me in place as she arched into my mouth. My fingertip lingered at her entrance enjoying the way she tried to lift her hips to get me to move.

When I rolled us on our side, I realized my mistake. Emily had my jeans undone with her hand shoved inside like some sort of goddamn Houdini. Her small hand wrapped around my dick nearly making me jump off the bed. I was hard, primed, and ready to come. A few strokes of her soft hand and I would blow. Time to put the brakes on.

"I need these off," I told her and tugged on her shorts.

With her hand now safely away from my dick,

she helped pull her shorts and panties down her long, toned legs. Neatly trimmed hair at the V of her thighs had my mouth watering. Her hands went to my tee pushing it up. I took over and pulled it over my head tossing it aside. Her eyes widened in appreciation, and her nails scraped over my chest down over my abs, stopping on my open jeans. I prayed to all things holy I would have the self-control not to fuck her tonight.

I rolled to my back, and Emily followed using her tongue to trace over where her nails had just scraped, stopping at my nipple to lick around it. She kissed every inch of my chest as I struggled to kick my jeans off, leaving my boxer briefs on. I needed the barrier; I was too weak. She was too tempting, too fucking sexy. Her hand was back inside my boxers fisting my dick.

"Em, slow down, baby," I begged, gently pushing her to her back. I came up on my elbow giving me the perfect view to fully take in her beautiful body. I had imagined what she looked like under her clothes thousands of times. The reality was so much better than the fantasy of her. Pretty raspberry-color nipples tightened under my stare. I ran my thumb across one watching it stiffen even harder.

"You're so beautiful," I whispered and lowered

my mouth, licking the outline of her puckered nipple before taking it back into my mouth. Emily's entire body went rigid when I pushed the tip of my finger into her wetness. Her legs closed around my hand, and I held still for a moment afraid I had done something wrong. After a few seconds, I whispered, "Spread your legs for me." She did, allowing them to fall limp on the bed. "You okay?" I asked between kisses over the swell of her breast.

"Yes," she moaned when I pushed in a little farther. "I'm okay."

Her hand pumped my dick faster, and she angled her head pressing kisses over my chest. Her lips on my skin... nothing fucking like it.

I pulled my finger out spreading her wetness up to her clit as she threw her head back on the pillow and moaned. I seized the opening and took her mouth in a bruising kiss. Working two fingers into her pussy, my thumb continued to rub circles over her clit. She rocked her hips up and jerked my dick in perfect rhythm with my fingers.

"If you don't want me to come in your hand, you have to stop," I warned her.

I was at the point of no return – I was going to come either way. I put more pressure on her clit and twisted my fingers in her pussy finding the spot I knew would have her screaming. Her answer was to firm her grip and stroke harder. The first pulsations started as her mouth opened in a silent scream. I kissed her hard and deep before any sound could come out and let go. I came in a violent rush of pure bliss, my come running over her hand onto her stomach.

I slowed my hand and gently ran my fingers over her folds, bringing her back down. With her hand still on my hard dick, she looked at me with wide eyes.

"Still?" she asked.

"You inspire me," I answered.

I didn't think now was a good time to tell her I could go two or three times in a night. While I had excellent recovery time, I usually needed a good work up to get hard again. I couldn't remember a time my dick was ready to go again this fast.

"Ignore it, he'll go down in a minute." I hoped.

"It's kinda hard to ignore," she said running her thumb over the head smearing come over the tip. "Lean down, I want to kiss you."

My dick having a mind of its own was thrilled with the turn of events. I was halfway to her lips when the loud shrill of my phone sounded. My eyes closed in frustration, and I rolled to my back to grab my phone off the nightstand.

Lenox.

This better be fucking good. "Yeah," I answered.

"Unfriendly inbound," Lenox said.

"Get dressed, baby," I whispered to Emily and rolled out of bed tagging my jeans off the floor, slipping them on, grabbing my holster next, and sliding it into place. Then to Lenox. "How long?"

"Now." He disconnected. Emily already had her shorts on and was pulling her shirt over her head. The sound of glass shattering splintered through the room.

"Fuck," I said at the same time Emily yelled, "Jason" and ran for the door.

I grabbed Emily around the waist and lifted her away from the door.

"I need you to trust me." I had seconds to make her understand. "Climb out your bedroom window and get into the Camaro and drive away. Do not stop, no matter what you see."

"Jason." She struggled.

"Now, Emily. Trust me. I need you safe so I can focus on Jason. Drive away anywhere, don't stop, just drive. There's a tracking device on the car. I'll find you. I promise."

I pushed the keys and my extra cell phone into her palm and closed her hand around them praying she would obey me.

Without waiting to see what Emily would do I rushed out the door closing it behind me. The living room was filling with smoke, and flames engulfed the curtains around the front window. Motherfucker.

I moved back down the hall to Jason's room. I opened the door and found him sitting up in bed with his knees pulled up to his chest.

"What was that?" he asked.

"There's a fire, bud, we have to go," I explained, picking him up from his bed. His little legs wrapped around my waist.

"Where's Mommy?" he cried.

"She's safe." There was no time to find something to put over his face, we needed to get the fuck out of the house.

I should've gone out his bedroom window, but I had to check Emily's room and make sure she did as I told her. I would never forgive myself if she was still somewhere in the house. I ran down the hall to Emily's room, and relief washed over me. The window was open, and the screen was pushed out. I sat on the windowsill and threw my legs over. A small jump and Jason and I were out of the house. I shifted Jason's leg and drew my Glock.

"Hold on to me tight, okay?" I whispered.

His arms and legs tightened. I stalked around the side of the house mindful that I had Jason's little body in front of mine. I hated that I didn't have any other options, he was safest in my arms.

Lenox met me on the side of the house and took the lead walking us to the front of the house. The Camaro was gone. Lenox's SUV was in the street still running, passenger side door open.

"Where's Levi?"

"Tailing Emily," Lenox answered as I got in the passenger seat still holding Jason. He slammed the door closed and rounded the hood.

"You okay, bud?" I asked.

"I'm scared. I want my Mommy," he answered with his face buried in my neck.

"I know. We're going to get her now. She's okay and waiting for you."

I tried to reassure him, but I had a bad fucking feeling that Lenox wasn't telling me something.

Lenox got in the SUV, and before I could ask him what was going on, Jason's head came off my shoulder, his hands went to my face, and with a surprising strength, he gripped my face.

"Do you promise?" His blue eyes that looked so much like his mother's bore into mine.

I was so proud of Jason – for not freaking out, for wanting to take care of his mom, for being so brave. With a renewed sense of purpose and the knowledge I could not let him down, I answered, "I promise."

His head went back to my shoulder, and I buckled the seatbelt around both of us.

Lenox was already out of Emily's neighborhood and speeding down the main road. The aftermarket GPS display had two dots blinking about twenty miles ahead of our location.

"Why is Levi following Emily?" I asked.

"Because Gains is following Emily," he answered.

I grabbed Lenox's cell out of the cradle and started to dial Emily.

"Don't bother, Levi's on with her. He's giving her directions to the shed. Clark and Connor are already there waiting for Gains and Emily.

Motherfucker. If Emily got hurt, it would be my fault. In my haste to get her away from the house, I unknowingly put her in more danger.

Hang in there, baby. We're right behind you.

I prayed that she could hear me.

CHAPTER FIFTEEN

Emily

Hands down, the hardest decision I had ever made was trusting that Jasper would take care of Jason. I smelled smoke and had to fight every motherly instinct not to rush to help my child. Jasper promised he would get Jason, and I had to trust him. If Liam was there, I'd rather him go after me than find Jason.

When the phone in my lap rang, I thought it was going to be Jasper telling me to turn around and come back to get them. Instead, it was Levi instructing me to stay calm, and he was going to give me directions where to go. When the car behind me sped up and bumped the car, Levi cursed a string of foul words and told me to speed up, explaining that it was Liam in the car behind me. Now here I was speeding down the highway with Liam following me and Levi following us both.

"You're doing great, Emily. Keep your speed steady. Lenox checked in, Jasper and Jason are both fine and heading our way." His announcement assuaged my worst fears. Thank God Jasper got him out. "Now, let's get you to the shed."

"Thank you," I said trying to stay focused on the road, but my relief was overwhelming, and it was hard to stay focused on the road.

"There's going to be a turn up here..."

Levi was cut off when Liam rear-ended me again, hard this time, making me lurch forward in the seat.

"Shit!" I yelled.

"Stay calm. There's a bend in the road, you have to drop your speed to take the curve. I want you to slow down by ten, downshift into fourth gear." I did as he instructed and the engine whined in protest. My RPMs revving higher than I'm sure Jasper would be happy about.

"I see the bend," I told him.

"Good. I want you to brake into the turn and accelerate out."

"Okay."

I started the turn, and then began to accelerate.

"Jam that bitch in fifth and gun it. Now."

I shifted into fifth and slammed my foot on the accelerator, the car shooting forward like a bat out of hell. This would've been exhilarating if I didn't have my crazy ex behind me trying to run me off the road.

"Perfect. You have approximately eight miles until the road bends left. Same thing, brake in, slam out. When you bank left, I might lose sight of you. After the bend, you'll be three miles from your turn off. On the right side of the road, you'll see mile markers. It's gonna be hard to see them – pay attention. Pass three. Right after the third one there will be a yellow marker on the right. Turn right down the dirt road with the yellow marker. Got it?"

"Yes," I answered, and prayed I could remember.

"Repeat it back to me," he demanded, as I sped down the road, the speedometer hovering over ninety miles per hour.

"Three-mile markers. Turn right at the yellow marker," I repeated.

"Perfect."

I had gained a good distance from Liam, and the left bend was coming up fast. I slowed my speed and took the turn. Hitting the gas once again I was almost to ninety.

"I've lost sight of you, tell me what you see?"

"First marker." A few seconds later. "Second marker."

"Drop your speed. You're almost there," he calmly told me.

"Third marker." I hit the brakes and saw the yellow marker. Fuck I was still going too fast. "Shit."

I made the turn, the car fishtailing. I fought to regain control on the narrow dirt road. There were trees on either side not giving me much room to maneuver. The car straightened out, and I slowly pressed the accelerator not wanting to go off the road.

"I made the turn," I announced.

"Great. The road dead ends in a half a mile. Keep your speed up."

"Rocks are flying up hitting the car," I complained.

"Fuck the car. Jasper's more worried about you. The car can be replaced."

I would examine Levi's words at a later time when I could enjoy the suggestion of his statement.

"I can see an old building. It has a white roof," I told him.

"Awesome. You did great. Gains blew by the turn-off, I'm staying with him. Don't hang up with me. I want to hear Clark or Connor before I go," he said.

"I don't know…"

"Stay strong. You're almost done."

I sucked back the tears that were threatening to fall and slowed the car, finally coming to a stop in front of the building. Connor and Clark both ran to the car. Connor opened the driver side door pulling me out, the phone falling off my lap on the ground.

"Shit. Wait a second, Connor." I bent down and picked up the phone hoping we hadn't lost the connection. "You still there?" I asked.

"Yes."

"I'm here, with the guys."

"Clark?" Levi asked.

"All clear here," he answered. "Lenox and Jasper are ten minutes out."

"Headed west on I-15. Lenox has the plate info," Levi told Clark.

"Copy that," Clark said.

"Wait. Don't hang up." I brought the phone closer to my mouth.

"Still here."

"Thank you, I couldn't have done it without you."

"Anytime, girl. You did great. Jasper will be proud. Out."

The phone went dead, and my legs went wobbly. Connor wrapped his arms around me and helped me inside the building. He sat us down on a tattered old, ugly couch that looked like it had been brought here after being found on the side of the road. I would've questioned how sanitary it was to sit on if I wasn't so shaky.

Clark came over with a bottle of water, and weirdly enough, a chocolate bar. I took the water and shook my head at the chocolate.

"Trust me, it will help with the adrenaline rush," he told me.

"Thanks." I took the chocolate bar and gulped my water. My mouth felt like I had eaten a handful of cotton balls.

Clark was on his phone pacing by the front door when I heard tires skidding on the gravel out front. Surely it couldn't have already been ten minutes?

The door slammed open, and Jasper stalked in, barefoot, no shirt, and my boy in his arms. There had never been a better sight, ever!

I jumped up and ran to meet them at the door. He took one arm off Jason and pulled me into them, hugging me close.

"Hey sweetheart, are you alright?" I asked Jason.

"I was scared," he said, wrapping one of his arms around me as well.

"I'm so sorry." I cried with my arms wrapped around both of them. "So, so, sorry."

We stood hugging for several minutes, Jasper whispering sweet words of encouragement into my hair. Everything from, *you were so brave* to *I'm so proud of you*. Finally, he kissed the top of my head and pulled back just enough to see my face. "Thank you for trusting me."

I was too overcome with emotion to answer him, instead on impulse I rolled up on my tippy toes and pressed my lips to his. I didn't care if the other guys saw. And while I should've cared if my son saw, I figured that the man had saved his life and Jason would understand.

"Let's get you two on the couch for a minute while I talk to the guys," Jasper suggested, moving us across the room.

"You can let go now, bud. You did great," Jasper said and kissed Jason on the top of his head.

Don't even think it. I kept repeating in my mind. But I couldn't stop myself – Jasper holding Jason, protecting him, comforting him – hope bloomed and spread taking over every faraway fantasy I'd ever had about finding a man to love me and Jason. A man like Jasper.

"You kept your promise," Jason said and kissed Jasper's cheek.

"A man always keeps his promises."

Jason crawled into my arms. He was safe. They were safe.

Jasper's hand grabbed the back of my head and kissed me. His was longer than the one I had given him. He let his lips linger on mine. "Things have changed," he said.

When I didn't say anything, he continued. "So damn proud of you both."

Jasper walked away leaving me stunned. What had changed? That was my thought as I sat on the couch. Between thanking God my son was safe, I was trying to puzzle out what he meant.

It didn't take long for Jason to fall asleep in my arms. I followed shortly thereafter drifting off knowing that Jasper was there. We'd be safe.

"EMILY," Connor's voice pulled me from sleep. "Sorry to wake you, we're getting ready to leave."

"I didn't mean to fall asleep. Where are we going?" I asked.

"You and Jason are going to Jasper's house."

"How's my house?" I was afraid of the answer. I think my insurance would cover the damage, however, it couldn't replace all my keepsakes. All of the memories.

"The front of the house is a total loss, smoke and water damage to the rest. I'm sorry, sweetie."

I closed my eyes thinking of all the things I could never replace. Fucking Liam, I hated him. "I'm not sure my insurance will cover crazy people fire-bombing my house," I whispered trying not to wake Jason.

"That doesn't matter. Jasper took care of that and called the Commander. A marker was called in with the Fire Chief. On record, the fire started because of faulty wiring. They don't want the police involved."

Jasper saved the day again. First, he puts his military career on the line, now he was asking people to commit perjury on my behalf.

"When will this end?" I asked, not really expecting an answer.

"Soon. You good going with Jasper?"

"Did he say he wants us going with him?" I asked.

"No. He said you and Jason *were* going with him. And if I tried to take you guys with me, he'd shoot me in the balls."

"No, he didn't." I smiled. That was mildly funny if he did actually say that.

"He did. I'd like to keep my balls, but if you'd rather come back with me, I can take one for the team." He laughed.

"I'd like to go with Jasper."

"I thought so. You did great tonight." I followed Connor's gaze and saw Jasper walking our way.

"I was scared shitless, but I admit the driving fast part at the end was kinda cool."

"Don't even think about it," Jasper said when he stopped in front of us.

"Think about what?" I asked trying to look as innocent as possible.

"Driving that fast again," he answered.

I wasn't going to argue with him about it now, but I would be driving the Camaro again.

"Sorry about your car. Is there a lot of damage?" I asked.

"Didn't look and don't care. All I care about is that you and Jason are safe."

There it was; Levi called it. He didn't care that his car was damaged.

We were more important.

The hope I was trying to stop, grew.

CHAPTER SIXTEEN

Jasper

I looked at a sleeping Emily and Jason in my bed. Jason lay half over his mother, her arms wrapped tightly around his little body. They looked peaceful in their slumber, their faces relaxed, so much love between the two of them. Thank God, they were safe. I've been on a lot of missions over the years, faced down a good number of terrorists, and other generally bad men. Guns have been held to my head, knives to my throat. I had watched Roman hold a gun to Lily and threaten to kill her. And never in any of those situations had I had a hard time keeping my heart rate and fear in check.

When I walked into Jason's room and saw him sitting on his bed, scared, something changed in me.

Knowing that Emily had trusted me enough to take care of the one person she loved most in this world changed something, too. Feelings and wants I had long ago buried came to the surface. I could no longer deny I was falling in love with her, and with her came Jason.

Levi had followed Gains out to the freeway but lost him. He was just as pissed as I was that Gains had gotten away. The kick in the ass was Levi could've overtaken Gains, however, not on a highway with innocent civilians around. It wasn't worth the risk of harming other drivers on the road, so Levi had slowed his speed and let Gains go.

When we caught up to that fucker, I was going to gut him. He'd never be an issue for them again. I closed my bedroom door and thought about all the things we needed to do tomorrow. Emily and Jason had lost pretty much everything. We'd have to stop by the mall and get them new clothes and Jason some toys. I looked in my spare bedroom; it had a bed and some stacked boxes in the corner, otherwise it was as barren and boring as the rest of my house.

Could I convince Emily to stay here with me? Was it too soon to ask her to move in with me? Fuck, but I didn't care if it was too fast, I was ready. Now that I had the one person that made me feel whole, one I could see a future with, I wasn't letting her go.

I went to the fridge – empty. Another thing we had to do tomorrow if Emily and Jason were going to be staying here. I needed something other than condiments and a six-pack. I grabbed a beer and popped the top. There were a few more hours until sunrise. It was going to be a busy day. The team had everything in place to take down Phillips. Once he was in lock-up, all efforts could be turned to Gains.

LEVI SHOWED up bright and early with a box of donuts, a gallon of milk, and a carton of orange juice.

"These are the best donuts ever," Jason exclaimed eating his second one.

"Slow down, bud. You're gonna give yourself a stomach ache." I laughed as Jason shoved more into his mouth.

"Manners," Emily chastised.

"Sorry," Jason grumbled.

I went back to the file Levi had brought over and scanned the new intel on Philips and Chuck, the bank manager.

"Did you know Chuck had a stepson in the Army?" I asked.

"He did? No, Chuck didn't talk much about his private life. I knew he was married only because he had a photo of him and his wife on the filing cabinet behind his desk. Sometimes he forgot to stand it back up after he was done..." Emily stopped herself from finishing.

"Done with what?" Levi questioned.

"If you're done eating why don't you go wash your hands and face," Emily told Jason.

She waited for Jason to push back from the table and leave the room before she continued.

"I hate to be a gossip and speak ill of the dead. But, it was pretty well known that he was cheating on his wife with Beverly. She'd go in his office, shut the door, and be in there for a long while. She'd also stay late. There were times after she left his office that the picture of him and his wife would still be face down. Like he had forgotten to stand the frame back up," Emily explained.

"Wait. Beverly Foster? She has a three-year-old daughter?" I asked.

"That's her. She was there, the day of the robbery," she confirmed.

I knew the name Beverly sounded familiar.

"Did she ever tell you who her daughter's father was?" Levi asked.

"No, never a name. She said he didn't want the baby, signed away his legal rights, and moved away," Emily said.

Levi was taking down notes about the love triangle, or foursome as it may be, that was getting more convoluted the more we dug.

"Did you ever meet Chuck's wife?" I asked.

"Once. She came in demanding to see Chuck. I checked that Beverly was at her station before I took her back. I hated covering up their affair. It was wrong, and I felt bad. However, I didn't want the woman going postal in a bank full of customers."

"Smart call," Levi said.

"Can I watch TV?" Jason asked walking back into the kitchen.

"Sure thing, let me help you," I said taking Jason into the living room.

I set him up on the recliner and showed him how to use the remote, and figured I needed to add buying a couch on the list of things to get done today. Two recliners wouldn't do.

"Thanks," he said.

I knelt down in front of him. "Everything okay?" I asked.

"I guess," he mumbled.

He wasn't okay.

"You can tell me, bud. What's wrong?" I prompted.

"I want my blanket and my bear," he told me.

Damn, Emily would've known to grab those things last night. I didn't even think that Jason would want to take something special with him out of his room. With the house on fire I was more concerned with getting him out. A dad would've known.

"I'll see what I can do about getting them for you this afternoon. If we can't get them, I'll take you to get something new." Then I thought about something I had in my office, something I bought when I pulled my head out of my ass and was going to go after Liz. "I'll be right back."

I grabbed the stuffed bear off my desk. I had seen it in the PX, and on a whim, I bought it. The bear was dressed in Army fatigues, complete with hat and boots. My heart ached for the child I had never met. For her mother that I turned my back on. "I'm so sorry Liz," I whispered to the room.

Jason was where I had left him on the recliner flipping through the channels. "Will this work for now?" I asked, handing him the bear.

His face lit up, and he took the bear. "This is so

cool. He's wearing ACUs." It was funny hearing a kid so young knowing the acronym for an Army combat uniform.

"Yep, and a pair of Oakley standard issue tac boots. Cool right?" I tapped the boots.

"Thanks, Jasper. He's awesome. I'll be careful with him, I promise."

"No worries, bud. He's yours."

Jason started playing with the bear, and I made my way back to the kitchen table, both Levi and Emily staring at me. What the hell?

"What?" I asked.

"Nothing," Levi said and went back to his file.

Emily continued to look at me, her eyes shiny. "Thank you."

"For?" I asked.

"Being so good to him."

I had fucked up with her so bad in the beginning that she was now thanking me for being nice to a little boy. I might have felt uncomfortable around kids because they reminded me of everything I had lost, everything I had pushed away and turned my back on, but I didn't not like kids. I wasn't some cock-sucker who would be mean to a kid.

"I filled her in on Captain Phillips," Levi

changed the subject. "Seems Phillips had been in the branch as well to take out a personal loan."

"To pay off his gambling debts, if I had to guess. I looked over his finances, too. Seems he blew through the money that Roman gave him monthly. Between paying off Beverly to be quiet, his gambling, and drug habit, he was stretched thin," I added.

"I really am oblivious; all of this was happening right in front of me, and I didn't even notice. Hell, I even thought you guys were in research and development." Emily's face got tight, and she shook her head.

"Why would you know? You had no reason to suspect anything was going on," Levi said.

"It's scary to think all of this was going on in my branch under my nose. It goes to show you really can't trust anyone."

I hoped I wasn't included in that blanket statement. Logically I knew she trusted me; she left me to take care of Jason, but there was still a nag in the back of my mind.

"Connor's on his way over," I told Emily. "He's gonna stay here with you and Jason while we take down Philips. It shouldn't take long. We're picking him up at his office."

"Do you think Liam will come after us again?" she asked softly.

"Yes," I answered. "I wish I didn't have to tell you this, but I need you to stay vigilant. Gains is dangerous. He's not going to stop until he has that book. I don't want you scared, just aware. You and Jason will be protected."

"Can't I give him the book and be done?" she asked.

"No. He needs to be gone, once and for all. Steven did a good job keeping him away all these years. Now he needs to be put down so he never comes after you two again."

"I don't want anything to happen to you." She was worrying her lip again, biting it, and I wanted to lean across the table and lick the sting of her bite away.

Last night had gone to shit. I had my girl naked in bed getting ready for round two when Gains showed up and literally blew that moment to hell.

"Nothing is going to happen to any of us. We know what we're doing," I told her.

"This isn't our first rodeo. Gains is child's play. An unruly child, but a child nonetheless. He won't be an issue for you much longer," Levi said.

My phone vibrated when I checked it was a text from Connor.

"Connor's here," I announced, getting up to answer the door. The man was growing on me. We had the same objective, keeping Jason and Emily away from Gains. He had proved to be smart and trustworthy.

"I checked the book like you asked. You were right; the numbers are bank account numbers. I ran a trace, seems Gains was paying off some rather important people. Not only in Petersburg, but the surrounding areas as well," Connor said as soon as I opened the door.

"Did any of the accounts match up to the accounts we gave you?" I asked.

Levi had given Connor a list of all known bank accounts and routing numbers to Roman's accounts, as well as Phillips, and the Army Specialist-turned-drug dealer Miller.

"No," he answered.

"Good." I opened the door wider letting him enter.

"Uncle Connor," Jason said and jumped up running to him.

A twinge of jealousy tingled my spine. It was irrational. Jason had known Connor his whole life.

But I wanted Jason's eyes to light up like that when I entered the room. I wanted him to run to me in excitement. Not Connor.

"Hey. What's that?" Connor asked, pointing to the bear.

"Jasper gave him to me. He's cool." I didn't know if Jason was referring to the bear or me. Either way, my heart swelled with...happiness.

"He is cool," Connor said, with a thoughtful expression.

It was time to go pick up Phillips. Before I left, I needed to talk to Emily. "A word?" I asked.

"Sure," she answered and followed me back to my bedroom.

I shut the door behind us and pushed her against the door, caging her in. She started to say something, but I silenced her with a kiss. I'd been dying to kiss her all morning. I needed my lips on hers, needed to remind her of our connection. The kiss quickly turned demanding, I angled her head for better access. I consumed her, holding nothing back. Not my passion, my want, my need for her, and most of all, not the love that had taken root.

I slowed the kiss before I took it too far. My hands were itching to touch her, feel her soft skin pebble under my fingertips, taste her sweetness.

"What's changed?" she asked against my lips.

It took me a minute to break out of the sexual fog and remember what she was asking. "Everything," I said, kissing the corner of her mouth. "I know I said I wasn't sure if I could make you promises. I was wrong." I kissed her again. "I want those promises between us." I deepened the kiss again, loving the way she melted into me. I pulled away and readied myself to say the words, ones I had never said to a woman, not even to Liz in all the years we had known each other. "I'm falling in love with you."

I felt rather than heard the sharp intake of her breath against my lips. "Me, too. I tried to stop it. I knew you weren't ready for us, but I couldn't," she admitted.

Thank fuck she felt the same way.

"I have to go. We'll talk more when I get home. I want you and Jason here, with me. Think about it. I know you have to do what you think is best for him, but you need to know, I want you guys in my house."

"Until I can find a new house?" she asked.

"No. For good. This goes where I hope to fuck it does, there's no point in you finding a place only to move back here."

"I'll think about it," she answered.

That would have to do for now. She needed to

think, and I had a scumbag to lock up. However, I would be thinking of ways to make her stay if she decided it was best for her to leave.

"Good enough. Be safe today. Please listen to Connor. We'll go to the mall and get you guys some stuff when I get home."

She nodded her head and smiled. "Okay, Jasper." Her smile, my name whispered from her lips was a direct shot to my gut. I wanted that smile directed at me, every day. "Please be safe."

"Always."

This fuckstick better go down easy and talk fast. I didn't have time to screw with Philips today. I wanted to get home to Emily and Jason. I wanted to be surrounded by their goodness. Now I understood why Lenox was always in such a rush to get home after a mission. He had something at home – love and family waiting for him.

I wanted that.

CHAPTER SEVENTEEN

Jasper

Clark, Levi, Lenox and I donned our uniforms for today's festivities and followed the Commander into the building where Captain Phillips worked. The staff sergeant that sat behind the desk jumped to attention calling out, "Attention on deck," when the Commander entered. With a snap of his head to the NCO, he continued to the stairs not bothering to announce the purpose of his visit.

Captain Phillips was sitting behind his desk when we entered his office.

"What the fu..." Phillips snapped at the interruption but quickly stood when he saw it was the Commander who had entered without knocking.

"Please, excuse my manners, Commander," Phillips recovered.

"Your manners? What mode of action would you like me to excuse?" the Commander asked.

"I'm not tracking, sir," Phillips responded, still standing at attention.

"No, I guess you wouldn't. Probably pretty hard to track when you're gacked out on coke, trying to hide your mistress and love child, and selling out your country, you motherfucking prick. Guess that's a full-time job in itself." Phillips reached down toward his desk drawer. Clark, Levi, Lenox and I all drew our sidearms and leveled them at Phillips. "Go ahead, you disgraceful piece of shit. I dare you," the Commander taunted.

Phillips wisely pulled his hand back and clasped them in front of him.

"Too bad. I was hoping this would be a short day. One of them shooting your treacherous ass would've sped things up. Clark, you get the pleasure. Escort this waste of space out to the car. Levi, stay here. Everything in the office is to be packed up. Lenox, Jasper do your worst, I'll meet you at the shed in an hour – that should be more than enough time. After all, he has no issues flappin' his gums like a whore in heat. And Jasper, don't be gentle."

The Commander had given me the green light to jack him up, but leave him breathing. Which was a shame, I would've liked to put him down.

Phillips didn't fight when Clark and I flanked him on the way to the car, Lenox a few steps ahead. No one spoke on the way to the shed, but that changed the moment he was pushed into the building.

"I can explain," he said.

"I'd love to hear this," Lenox said as I yanked his name tape off his uniform and threw it on the floor.

I went about removing all insignia patches off his uniform; he didn't deserve to wear the flag, rank, and unit symbols of the Army on his ACUs. He was a traitor. His actions had put U.S. lives in danger.

"Roman was going to kill my daughter," he cried. Yes, actual tears leaked from his eyes.

"What intel did you pass to Roman?" Lenox started, uncaring that the man was trying to excuse his behavior.

"He was going to kill her," Phillips repeated.

"You mean the child you turned your back on, the child you didn't want? The child that you threw away and paid her mother not to tell your wife? That child?" Lenox screamed in his face. "What intel did you pass?"

Lenox's words might have been for Phillips, but they hit me like a Mac truck. I was no better than Phillips, I had done all those things, too.

"Dates and locations of arms drops. Battalion movements. Any information I could dig up about deployment dates on the 707."

"What'd you give him on the 707?" Clark asked.

"Practically nothing. The only access I had was when the 707 was auditing bases. Roman wanted to know when the 707 went out for an audit. I guess he didn't want you guys catching on to the arms drops, the guns and munitions never made it in theatre so they couldn't be returned."

What a dumb fuck.

"The bank robbery?" I asked.

Phillips paled. He seemed to be more worried about the robbery than Roman.

Clark pulled out his phone and scrolled down the screen a few times before he put it back in his pocket and asked, "What was the trade-off with Miller?"

Phillips didn't answer.

"Choose your next statement carefully. Jasper hasn't had any fun since he took out your friend in the bank, and he's itchin' to get a piece of you. You see, there's a code we live by – loyalty, honor, fidelity,

God, and country. You seem to like to disrespect all those things."

Still nothing out of Phillips. Clark nodded my way, and with a well-practiced move, I pulled him close with my left hand, and a strong jab to his solar plexus had him coming off his feet before he doubled over in pain.

"We can do this all day," Clark explained.

Phillips tried to inhale and held his stomach. "He was..." He stopped to suck in a breath "He was gonna take out Beverly." Piece of shit was going to have the mother of his child murdered. "She has been threatening to tell my wife for a long time. She's pregnant again and said that she wanted us to be a family.

Phillips was still bent forward, his hands on his knees. Rage taking over, I kneed him in the face, satisfied when I heard the sickening sound of bone breaking, and he fell on his ass with the force of the blow.

"Did you ever take into consideration maybe the baby was Chuck's?" I asked.

"She was fucking both of you. Two married men fucking the same woman. Downright disgraceful," Clark added.

"Who else have you sold information to?" Lenox asked.

"No one. Once word that Roman had been killed got out, I thought I was off the hook," Phillips said.

Lenox pulled out his phone and put it to his ear. "Where do you want this POS? I'm done breathing the same air as him." Lenox was silent for a moment then a broad smile crossed his face. "Roger that." Then to us. "To the airfield, boys."

"No. I have rights under the UCMJ rules and the Geneva convention," Phillips argued.

"Unfortunately, you're right. Even a piece of shit like you has rights afforded by the very country you betrayed. Don't worry, I'm sure you'll be appointed legal counsel when you arrive at your destination," Lenox told him.

"No, I won't. You know I won't. Turn me over to the MP. I'll admit to everything," he begged.

"I know no such thing. Now would be the time where you shut the fuck up," Clark told him.

Philips struggled all the way to the car, making us drag him out of the car as well all the way to the airplane where we handed him over to two men in plain clothes, no identification, no names. Whatever agency they belonged to, Phillips was their problem now.

Good riddance.

My only thought was getting back to my house to see Emily. I didn't like that Gains was out there somewhere, no doubt plotting his next attack. The fucker was next. He was going down, and for good.

CHAPTER EIGHTEEN

Emily

Jasper had been gone for hours, and while it was nice spending time with Connor and Jason, I was tired of watching TV and I was hungry.

I had begged Connor to take us somewhere, but he refused until Jason said he was hungry, too. He agreed to take us to a drive thru. It's funny how you can spend all day lazy around the house not caring, but when you're told you can't leave, all you want to do is get out of the house – even for fast food.

I was happy to get in the car. With Jason in such close proximity that meant Connor had to stop drilling me about my relationship – if that's what you wanted to call it – with Jasper. He was a close friend, but I didn't feel comfortable talking to him about

Jasper. Not yet anyway, not while Jasper and I were still trying to figure things out. It felt like a betrayal to Jasper. I would never tell Connor about Jasper's past, and without fully explaining that, I couldn't explain why he had a *sudden change of heart*, to use Connor's words about Jason.

I knew Connor was worried about us, and I tried to reassure him. He admitted that he liked Jasper and thought he was a strong, decent man; however, he was concerned that Jasper would break my heart. He may have been right, Jasper had the power to destroy me. However, I was willing to take my chances.

Nothing ventured, nothing gained.

"What do you guys want to eat?" Connor asked when he pulled onto the main highway going toward the base.

"I want nuggets," Jason said from the backseat. His second favorite food behind pizza.

"I'm good with whatever," I told him.

Connor stopped at the next fast food restaurant and went through the drive thru. I looked into the bag and realized they forgot the dipping sauce. Connor pulled into a spot. "Sorry, I don't think Jasper even has ketchup at his place," I said.

"It's fine. Stay in the car with the door locked. I'll be right back." Connor started to open the door.

Before he could protest, the door was wrenched all the way open, and a loud bang exploded in the car. Blood poured from Connor's stomach, and I struggled out of my seatbelt trying to get to the back seat when the back door was opened. Jason was pulled to the door, a gun pointed at his head.

"I wouldn't move, Emily. You bring me my book or Jason dies," Liam said.

"Don't do this, Liam. Take me, please leave Jason alone," I cried.

He threw a scrap of paper in the backseat. "Call me when you have the book. Don't think about sending Army boy or I'll kill Jason. It's you with my book, or you never see him again."

"Please," I screamed frozen in place as Liam held a gun to my little boy's head. Jason's eyes were full of tears, and he was trembling. "PLEASE!"

Liam took off running with Jason, and I got out of the car. I was afraid to chase him and have him kill Jason there in the parking lot. Connor was shot, and Liam had Jason.

"No, no, no," I yelled, and my legs gave out. I didn't register the pain when my bare knees made contact with the asphalt. What was I supposed to do? A crowd had gathered around the car. I heard the wailing of sirens in the distance, someone was talking to me, but I couldn't hear what they were saying.

All I could hear was Liam's words roaring in my ears. *I'll kill him.*

Jasper

There were police cars surrounding a fast food joint not too far off post. Lenox had to slow the SUV once we got close, partly due to looky-loos and because the fire trucks, police, and ambulances had a lane blocked off.

I looked in the parking lot to see what all the commotion was and my blood turned to ice.

"Stop. That's Connor's car," I yelled.

His red sports car was unmistakable. Lenox veered off the road and slammed on his brakes. He wasn't fully stopped before I jumped out of the car and ran toward the scene. An officer tried to stop me, but I rushed past him through the police tape. "That's my wife," I yelled.

Connor was on the ground with multiple EMTs surrounding him. Emily was on her knees screaming, but I couldn't make out what she was saying. I skidded to a halt in front of her, dropping to my knees, uncaring I had basically knocked an officer out of the way in the process.

"Where's Jason," I asked.

"Gone. He took him," she cried and launched herself at me knocking me on my ass, clinging to me like a spider monkey. For the second time in the same number of minutes my life crashed down around me.

I didn't have to ask *who*. I knew Gains had Jason.

"Em, I need you to calm down a minute and tell me everything that happened, baby. Step by step."

I heard Lenox and Clark push back the local police officers, telling them that Connor was a Deputy US Marshal and lying saying Emily was a protected witness. I didn't need the PD getting in my way.

"He shot Connor and grabbed Jason. He said he wanted me to bring him the book. If I didn't, he'd kill Jason. He threw a phone number in the backseat."

"Good. Which way did he go? Did you see what type of car he got into?" I asked.

"He ran around the building. I didn't follow him," she cried.

"You did the right thing."

I looked at Lenox. His face was hard, and his eyes looked ready to shoot fire. He seemed to understand my struggle. He gave me a chin lift, and in a defining moment, I knew what I had to do.

"Listen to me. You're gonna stay with Lenox and Clark. They know what to do and won't leave your side. I'm gonna go get Jason," I told her.

"No." She held on to me tighter. "He said not you, only me with the book. He'll kill him."

"You have to trust me again. I promise you, swear to God, I will find Jason and bring him home to you. But you have to stay with the guys." She still wasn't convinced. "Em, I will protect him with my life, you have my word."

She nodded her head, and Lenox pulled her off me allowing me to stand.

"You don't have to say it, I know," Lenox said.

"I called it in," Clark said.

I was trusting my team to keep her safe.

I pulled Emily out of Lenox's arms and hugged her tightly. With a kiss on her forehead, I passed her back and took off in a full sprint back to the SUV.

I called Levi. "Where am I going?" I asked when he answered.

"He headed north on Washington Boulevard," he said.

I drove to the next spot where I could make a U-turn and headed north.

"Traffic cameras are only going to get us so far. Once he gets off the main roads, we're fucked. There are no cameras on the country roads."

"Aren't you a ball of fucking good news," I snapped.

He wasn't telling me anything I didn't already know, I just didn't want to hear how FUBAR'd the situation was. I had to find Jason.

"Left on First," Levi said ignoring my outburst. I had about three miles until my turn.

"Any idea where he would take Jason? Any known associates in the area?" I asked.

"Phillips' house is in the opposite direction, though he could've double backed using back roads. I'm still sorting through traffic cams. Miller lived on base, he wouldn't go there. No one else that I could find."

"On First, where to?" I asked.

"Last cam has him on Battlefield, make a right," Levi said.

"What's off Battlefield besides the campground?"

There was a large military campground in the woods to the west. There was no way he'd go there. The campground was patrolled and well lit.

"I pulled up the satellite. Half a dozen private

homes, directly off the road. Farther back there are a few hunting cabins. They shouldn't be in use, it's offseason for deer hunting."

"He's in one of those," I told him. "Satellite image show any cars in front of a cabin?" I asked.

"No visual. I can barely make out the rooftops with the tree canopy," he answered. "It will take an hour at least to get a drone in the air with thermal."

That would be extremely helpful. We could easily see their heat signatures.

"Get one up," I told him.

"Text me your coordinates for standby."

"Roger," I acknowledged.

I turned off a dirt road and pulled as far as I could into the brush trying to conceal the SUV. I got out and shut the door.

"Where are you going?" Levi asked knowing I wasn't waiting like he had asked.

"Hunting."

CHAPTER NINETEEN

Emily

I was going out of my mind. Two goddamn days in a row my son had been in harm's way. TWO! Liam better pray that Jasper finds Jason safe or I'll kill him. I've never hated another human being as much as I hated him.

"Emily, stop pacing. Come sit down," Clark said.

I bit back the *fuck you* I wanted to say. Instead, I ignored him. It wasn't his fault Liam had Jason, but I was not in the right frame of mind to talk to anyone but Jasper. My cell phone was in my hand waiting for his call. I prayed it would be soon. It had been hours. HOURS! Liam could've been doing God knew what to my child.

It was torture. I was in the deepest pits of hell.

The phone in the hospital waiting room rang, and Lenox answered. It was only a few seconds later, and I could hear him saying thank you before he hung up.

"Connor's still in surgery," Lenox told me.

I should've been more concerned about Connor than I was. My mind was completely focused on Jason; there was nothing left to give Connor.

"I know..."

"What do you know, Lenox?" I spit out, my venom finally overflowing. "Do you know what it feels like to have your child held at gunpoint in front of you, then taken while you stood there and did nothing. Do you?"

"I was going to say, I know this is hard, but you need to stay hydrated. Adrenaline and dehydration are not your friends." Lenox held up a bottle of water. "While I don't know what it feels like to see my child at gunpoint, I know what it feels like to see a deranged terrorist hold a gun to Lily's head. A man who had killed countless people, including his own wife. I know a little about that fear, yes. Those moments where you see your whole world in danger, afraid they're going to die. I get that you're scared and you need to lash out. I'm a strong man, Emily, I can take it. You wanna punch and kick and scream?

Do it. But, you gotta know, Jasper's out there doing everything humanly possible to find Jason. He's a good tracker, smart, and he will get Jason. You have to drink something before you pass out. Jasper will kick my ass when he gets back if you have a bump on your head. He's already gonna go ballistic when he sees how torn up your knees are, and you've refused to allow us to clean them."

"I'm sorry. Fuck, I don't know what I'm supposed to be doing. I feel helpless sitting here. I'm an asshole for only thinking about Jason while Connor's fighting for his life."

"You're doing exactly what Jason needs you to be doing. Sitting here safely so Jasper can concentrate and get him. Right now, Jasper knows you are being taken care of; he's gone from the Jasper you know to the Special Operator. He has one objective – retrieve his hostage and take out the enemy."

Hostage, gunpoint, kidnapping, firebombs, GSW, critical – all words that are not in my daily vocabulary yet here I was hearing them over and over again. Police officers, fire chiefs, perjury, and fraud – again not normal things I deal with in my life. Yet I have lied to the police, the fire department, and my insurance company.

All because of Liam Gains. Lenox, Clark, Levi,

and Jasper had all put their jobs on the line because of me. Connor died, he *died*, in the ambulance on the way here and had to be resuscitated. I hoped Jasper tore the son of a bitch apart.

"Drink." Lenox handed me the bottle of water.

And that's how the next few hours went. I paced, Lenox handed me a water bottle every few minutes and made me drink more.

By the time the phone rang in the waiting room again, I was exhausted and I had to pee.

"Thank you," Lenox said and hung up the phone. Then to the room. "Connor's out of surgery. They repaired the damage and were able to remove the bullet. He'll be moved to ICU in a few hours. We can go up then."

Fatigue and relief in equal measure washed over me. He wasn't out of the woods, but he made it through surgery – that was something.

"Someone grab her a soda and a chocolate bar with peanuts," Lenox asked.

"I'm not hungry," I argued.

The last thing I wanted was to eat.

"I know you're not. I'm trying to keep you upright, not feed you. What you need is some real food and to lie down. But I know you won't do that."

"Thanks," I whispered. "I'm sorry."

"Stop apologizing. We've got your back, Emily."

Where the hell was Jasper? The guys told me he went dark, meaning he had cut off all communication in order to find where Liam was hiding. He hadn't checked in in a long time. What if something happened to him, too? I would never recover if I lost Connor, Jasper, and Jason.

Never.

Jasper

The sun had finally set, and I was in position. The house was situated as such I couldn't approach without there being shadows cast on the west, even with the trees. The east side was floor-to-ceiling windows and no cover on the north and south. I had no choice but to sit and wait.

My last communication with Levi was him confirming that Liam was in the house. The drone had shown two heat signatures, and the satellite had picked up Liam when he went out to get a box out of a shed that was in a clearing. Thank God for modern technology. I checked my phone was completely powered down one last time and touched my HK on my hip.

The cabin was small, one room. According to planning and zoning, there was a kitchenette and a bathroom. No other rooms were partitioned off. That didn't mean shit though; the owner could've built something after the final inspection. As much as I hated relying on intel that had not been confirmed, I had no choice.

I peeked in the side window and saw Jason sitting on the floor his back to the wall with what looked like an old-school Gameboy in his hands. I couldn't see if he was injured, but he was breathing – that's all that mattered. Gains was pacing the floor. I had no choice but to break the door down and pray it wasn't boarded on the other side. It was a calculated risk with no gear that would allow me to go through the window uncut. It was my only option.

I shouldered the door hard and fast, it opened and splintered under my weight. I rushed Gains and put him in a headlock from behind, lifting him off his feet. I reached into the waistband of his jeans, found his gun, and tossed it aside. I caught movement out of the corner of my eye, and saw Jason standing there, his eyes wide in fear.

"Everything's fine, bud. I need you to close your eyes and cover your ears. Hurry," I yelled.

Gains was struggling and kicking my shin, it hurt

like a son-of-a-bitch. I wasn't applying enough pressure to choke him out, I wanted the fucker awake when he died.

In a split-second decision, I opted against my gun. Shooting a .45acp in this small space would be deafening, not to mention the shot would've been heard for miles. I yanked my knife out of my uniform pocket and flipped the blade open.

"You fucked with the wrong boy," I said and sank the blade of my knife into the side of his neck. "See you in hell." With a twist of my blade, the last of his air left his body, and I let him fall to the ground.

Without thinking, I rushed to Jason and scooped him up. The moment I did, I wished I had taken off my uniform blouse. My hand and shirt had Liam's blood all over them.

"Are you hurt?" I asked.

"I'm scared." Jason started to cry in my arms.

"I know you are, bud. You're safe now. But are you hurt anywhere?" I asked again.

"No."

"Good. We're going home."

I ran half a mile before I stopped to pull my phone out.

"Update?" Levi asked.

"Done. I need clothes for both of us and a gallon of water for clean-up."

"Copy that." Levi disconnected.

"Almost there. You're doing great."

Jason didn't answer, but he held on tight as I ran us another three miles back to the SUV.

Jason was safe.

Liam Gains was dead. He'd never touch them again.

CHAPTER TWENTY

Emily

Connor was in his room in ICU. The doctor explained that he was still in critical condition and it would be touch and go through the night. They had to repair his liver, stomach, and remove his gallbladder. He was lucky - the bullet had barely missed his spine. We were allowed to visit him one at a time for five minutes only.

I looked in on him from the other side of the glass wall, his door was closed silencing the beeping and whooshing sounds the machines keeping him alive made. He looked horrible – like he'd been shot in the gut.

Please, God, let him be okay. I can't lose him, too.

"Emily, I need you to come with me," Lenox said, "Clark will stay here with Connor."

"Is everything okay?" I asked. "Is it Jason?"

"Everything's great. Come on."

Lenox hurried us to the elevator and ushered me in. "We didn't want to bring Jason up here."

"He's here? Jasper got him?" I was shaking so badly Lenox pulled me to his side before I lost my balance.

"He's here," Lenox confirmed. "I told you Jasper would bring him back."

"Is he hurt?"

"No."

Thank you, God!

The elevator dinged, the door opened, and Lenox walked us out of the hospital. Thankfully Lenox was holding me up, or I would've fallen to the ground.

There they were, once again Jason was wrapped around Jasper. He stalked toward me, his eyes never leaving mine. They were assessing and dangerous. He did a full body scan, and when he took in my knees his nose flared, and he shot a look at Lenox before they came back to me. He stepped into my personal space, hooked an arm around me, and pulled me out of Lenox's arms and into his.

He held us while I cried and mumbled unintelligible words, and sobbed some more. I was so overcome with emotion I couldn't catch my breath enough to ask any questions. I peppered Jason's little face with kisses, unable to stop myself from touching him. He was here, he was unharmed – we'd work through the rest.

"Connor?" Jasper asked over my head.

"Stable but critical," Lenox replied.

"She eat anything?"

"Not a thing," Lenox tattled on me. How did either of them expect me to eat food while my son was missing? What was it with food?

"Copy. We're going home," he said.

"We can't leave," I protested. "Connor's up there."

"Yeah, he is. And he'll be there in the morning. Baby, I just spent the last eight hours stalking through the woods. I'm emotionally wrecked. I want to take my woman home, clean her fucking knees up, get her and my boy into bed, wrap my arms around both of them, and sleep for a week."

I'd let the *fucking* go in front of Jason, just this once. But only because he called me his woman and Jason his boy.

"Okay." Now that I got myself under control

enough to talk I pushed Jason's hair off his forehead and gave him a kiss. "I love you, baby boy."

"I missed you, Mommy."

"I missed you, too. You ready to go home?" I asked.

I was afraid to ask him anything about his time with Liam. I needed to be sitting with my boy in my arms before I could handle hearing what happened.

"To Jasper's house, right?" Jason asked.

"Yeah, baby. Is that okay?" I asked.

"Jasper? You're not gonna leave us, are you?" Jason asked,

"I'm not going anywhere, bud. I promise." He kissed the top of Jason's head.

"Thanks, man," Jasper said to Lenox.

"No need."

"I'm sorry I was so crazy. Thank you for all your help." I pulled away from Jasper and wrapped my arms around Lenox, giving him a hug and a kiss on the cheek. Lenox squeezed me back and let me go. "You better get going. Your man looks impatient," he whispered.

"Let's go home." Jasper hooked me around the middle and walked us to the parking lot. Well, Jasper walked, I floated. I was on cloud nine. Jason was home, and hopefully, we'd get good news about Connor soon.

***

JASON WAS quiet on the drive home. I sat with him in the backseat after I pried him out of Jasper's arms. Seems that neither of them wanted to let go of each other. However, Jasper had to drive, and I wanted to hold my son.

I carried him into the house, and he stayed on my lap while Jasper cleaned the gravel and blood off my knees. Once they were cleaned, they didn't look that bad, a few scrapes that would scab over and heal in a few days. The physical proof of Jason's kidnapping would be gone long before the emotional bruises would be. I could only pray that those, too, would scab over and heal and not turn into lasting scars.

I tried to ask Jason a few questions, but he wouldn't answer. Jasper softly told me to be patient; Jason was still in shock and it would take time for him to open up. We piled into Jasper's bed. Jason curled into my front, Jasper at my back. He had his strong arms wrapped around both of us, blanketing us with his protection.

After Jason had fallen asleep, Jasper told me how

he'd found where Liam was holding Jason, why he had to wait so long, and finally what Jason had been doing in the cabin when he broke in. I'd finally mustered up the courage to ask the question that was on my mind since I first saw them at the hospital.

"Why is Jason in different clothes?" I held my breath waiting to hear Jasper's answer. He'd said that he found Jason unharmed. But that didn't explain why my son had changed clothes.

"There was blood on his clothes. I didn't want him in bloody clothes, and I didn't want you to see him like that."

"Where are you hurt?" I asked.

"It wasn't my blood."

"Will you tell me?" I asked.

Jasper was quiet for a moment then asked, "Do you want to know?"

"Yes," I answered. I wasn't sure I wanted details, but I had to know if Liam would come after us again.

"He's dead."

That was it – no elaboration, no apology, no remorse in his tone. Very matter of fact. I wondered if this was the Special Operator Jasper that Lenox was telling me about. The Jasper who had to be cold and detached.

"Thank you."

I wasn't sure what kind of human being it made me, but I was happy Liam was dead. The only thing I was sorry about was Jasper had Liam's death on his conscience.

Jasper kissed the back of my head and spooned in closer. "Let's get some sleep, yeah?" he asked.

"Yeah."

It was many hours before I fell asleep in Jasper's arms. My mind raced with the events of the last two days. What all of this meant for me and Jasper, Jasper and Jason, and for the three of us. I still hadn't answered Jasper's question about moving in. Jasper said he was ready to make promises. However, there was still a nagging feeling in the back of my mind. Something that Jasper had said to me was giving me pause. He had looked into Liz and Alesha's medical records, but he never said if he had faced her family or if he had visited them. I was afraid there was a hole in his heart, and he was using me as a Band-Aid instead of finding the closure he needed.

CHAPTER TWENTY-ONE

Jasper

It had been a week since Gains took Jason. A good week, no actually it'd been a great week. Emily was still working through some issues with not wanting Jason out of her sight, but she was getting better. It had taken some convincing to let him go back to school. After I pushed her, she finally broke down crying telling me her fears. After I reassured her that Gains was gone and would never touch Jason again, she allowed him back to school. We had a similar situation with Jason sleeping by himself.

We did go to the mall, and the furniture store, and the grocery store. I dropped a mint on new living room furniture and a bedroom set for Jason. Now that they were here, we needed more than two recliners. Emily helped pick out a large sectional and some crap to go on the walls. After the second time she asked my opinion on what she called wall art, I informed her that she was in charge of such items. I would handle the garage, grill, general maintenance, and clean up – the décor and the rest of the house were hers.

She refused to allow me to buy her and Jason new clothes. After a lengthy discussion, I knew I wasn't going to win and wisely shut my mouth on the issue. I did, however, put my foot down when it came to the groceries. We were learning, compromising, and it felt fucking wonderful. I admit I waited for the pinching in my gut when the one-week mark hit. As fucked up as it was, I hadn't been with a woman for over a week since high school. The day came and went, and all I felt was a deepening connection, a gratefulness I'd had them in my life.

Jason was doing great. Emily got him to open up about what happened. Hearing it through his eyes made me wish I had spent a little more time pushing my blade into Gains' throat and twisting slower. Jason said that he was scared, but Gains wasn't mean to him and hadn't hurt him in any way. When they got to the cabin, Gains basically handed him a video game and told him to sit and wait for his mom to come and get him.

Lenox and Lily had invited all of us over for a barbeque and poker. Jason was ready sitting on the couch playing on the tablet I had bought for him. Emily refused to acknowledge that it was Jason's and referred to it as mine, saying I was *letting* Jason play with it. Whatever made her feel better – it was Jason's. But I wasn't going to split cunt hairs over it. I was learning – picking my battles.

I went back to the bedroom to see what was taking Emily so long. We were already ten minutes late. I found her staring at herself in the mirror.

She looked fucking gorgeous in a knee-length sundress, her long silky black hair braided over one shoulder exposing the other. She was a goddamn miracle. I couldn't stop, better yet, I didn't want to stop myself when I walked up behind her wrapping my arms around her middle and kissing her exposed neck. She angled her head giving me better access, and I wondered if she'd kick my ass if I gave her a hickey. I wanted to. I wanted to suck and bite her soft skin and mark her for everyone to see. Mine.

"That feels so good," she moaned.

I loved that sound. We still hadn't moved past the making out and touching stage yet. Anytime she tried to go further, I put the brakes on. I barely let us round third base. The hand jobs and kissing and fingering were crazy good. Getting to know her body and feeling her hands touch me drove me to the point of insanity. Each time I had stopped us from going any further was torture. Sweet anticipation.

It was time.

"Tonight," I whispered against her shoulder kissing her there. "You'll be saying the same thing when I slide inside of you." I watched in the mirror as her eyes fluttered shut and her body trembled. "Do you like that idea?"

"Yes."

"What were you thinking about when I came in?" I asked.

Her eyes came open, and she smiled. "How happy I am."

I reached over and shut the door. Turning her in my arms, I picked her up and sat her on the vanity spreading her legs to accommodate my large frame between them.

I kissed her deep and sound, laden with hunger and promise. When I pulled away, her lips were red and wet, so much like other parts of her body when I was done.

"You think you can give me one quick one?" I asked.

Her beautiful blue orbs glazed over with need. "The question is, can *you* give me a quick one?"

Game on.

"You better grab that hand towel," I told her.

"Why?"

"You're gonna need something to muffle your scream. You won't have my mouth to swallow your pleasure. It's gonna be a little busy."

Her eyes flared, and she tried to tighten her legs around me.

"Oh no, baby, spread 'em. I'm hungry."

I quickly locked the bathroom door and got to my knees. I draped her legs over my shoulders and pushed her panties to the side.

With the first lick, I was drunk with desire. She tasted so damn good. My tongue teased at her entrance, and my thumb lightly grazed her clit.

"Oh my God," she mumbled.

My last thought before I went to work devouring her pussy was I hoped she remembered the towel. Because I was going to tongue fuck her like she'd never been before.

It might have been minutes, hell it could've been an hour, but when she exploded on my tongue, the evidence of her orgasm dripping down my chin, all I wanted to do was start all over. She writhed and ground herself against my mouth taking everything she wanted. It was so fucking sexy I could feel the wet spot of pre-come in my boxers. All it would take was one touch, and I'd shoot off like a schoolboy.

I stood up and wiped my face with the hand towel before I kissed her again. I pulled back remembering we had to go.

"Don't change your panties," I instructed.

"What? Why not? They're all wet."

"I know they are. I want you in wet panties. I want you to think about me licking your sweet pussy all day. And baby, when we get home tonight, I am gonna fuck you senseless, and after that, I'm gonna lay you down and love you the rest of the night."

With one last peck on the lips, I opened the door and left her standing there to think about what I said. The thought had crossed my mind to brush my teeth. However, I wanted the taste of her on my lips.

CHAPTER TWENTY-TWO

Emily

"So, you and Jasper, huh?" Lily asked as soon as she could corner me alone.

I couldn't help the smile that had formed. My plan was to play it cool, not show how head-over-heels in love I was with him. However, at the first mention of his name I failed miserably.

We were sitting on her back deck, watching Jason play with baby Carter on a blanket in the grass. I couldn't believe how much Carter had grown in the last month.

"He's getting so big. Have you started planning his first birthday party yet?" I asked.

"You're deflecting." She laughed.

Okay, I was. But not for the reasons she thought.

"I feel like it's too good to be true," I explained.

"How good is it?" She dropped her voice and leaned in close.

"I wouldn't know."

"What?" she screeched.

"Shhh. I mean, we've fooled around, and that's good-good. But we've never, I mean, we haven't... you know, had sex," I whispered. My face heated, and it had nothing to do with the beautiful weather and sunny skies.

"Wow."

"What do you mean, wow? Didn't you hear me? There's been no nookie, no home run, no knockin' the boots."

Lily tossed her head back and laughed. I didn't see what was so funny. She had to have been getting some from Lenox. He didn't strike me as the type of man who would go too long without. Not that I often thought about Lily and Lenox's sex life. It was merely an observation on my part.

"I'm gonna be real honest here. I was worried at first. The first night you met Jasper I told Shane that if Jasper tried to make you a flavor of the week I was gonna chop off his balls. He's a great guy, but he has..."

"I know what happened. He told me," I said, saving her the trouble of trying to explain Alesha to me without breaking his confidence.

"He told you?" Lily asked, surprised.

"He did. Before anything happened between us. He wanted me to understand why he'd pulled away at first. He also made it very clear in the beginning that he wanted to try but didn't know if he could make me promises. Since that first talk, things have changed. Promises have been made, but still no sex."

I sounded like I was some horny sex-depraved trollop.

"It's not about not having sex," I explained. "Sometimes I worry that it's me. I mean, I know about his past, he was very open about that, too," I grumbled. I hated thinking about all the women he'd been with. "He used to meet a woman at a bar, take her home, have sex."

"It is *you*," she said, and my heart sank. "*You* are different than the barflies he used to bring home. *You* are special to him. I'm proud of him for taking his time with you. Sweetie, you're not a one-weeker to him, you're his lifer."

"I don't know about all that. Thank you for telling me that. He keeps saying it, but you know when your feminine insecurities take root it's hard to shove them aside. I'm really, really happy. I'm falling in love with him." I admitted. "Actually, I think I've already fallen. And that worries me."

"It's not too good to be true, Emily. It's just damn good. And true. Enjoy it," Lily said on a smile.

"Is it crazy, I feel like a silly teenager and want to dance around because I've landed the hottest, strongest, smartest guy in the room?" I giggled. Yes, I giggled, like a teeny-bopper.

"I wouldn't go that far, sister. I might have to fight you on who got the hottest and strongest." Lily joined in laughing with me.

I had missed her so much, missed this.

"What are you two women laughing about?" Jasper's smooth sexy voice floated over from the back door.

"Nothing," we said in unison and busted out laughing once again.

Damn, it felt good to laugh.

"Dude, I think you and Lenox are screwed," Clark said shouldering his way past Jasper. "I bet they're comparing notes. You know... size does matter boys."

"Yeah, you'd know all about size mattering. I thought I saw some penis enhancement cream in your locker, how's that working out for you?" Jasper shot back.

"I don't know pretty boy, you wanna come find out for yourself?" Clark deadpanned.

"So help me God, if you two idiots are discussing the size of your cocks in front of my wife, I'm gonna junk punt you both," Lenox added, joining us outside.

"Don't mind me over here," Lily smiled at Lenox. "I know yours is the biggest, honey."

Three sets of jaws hit the ground before they picked them back up and roared with laughter. My shy innocent friend just made a dick joke. She was normally the one telling them to stop the obscenities, and here she was joining in.

"That was goddamn funny, Lily," Jasper said.

"Good woman right there. I love you, Lillian."

I loved that Lenox was demonstrative toward his wife. He didn't care if the guys were around, he touched and kissed her often, and had no issue with the guys hearing him tell her he loved her. Lenox had told me something in the hospital about how he had watched someone hold a gun to Lily's head. I wondered if that was why he didn't care that other people saw how much he loved his wife because he'd almost lost her.

"Who's ready for some poker?" Clark asked.

"Are we gonna wait for Levi and Connor to get here?" Jasper asked.

"Levi can't make it. Family shit. He had to go home for a few days," Lenox explained, and I watched as all three men's mouths flattened in annoyance. "Connor said that he had a date, but would be over for drinks when he was done."

"A date?" I asked, I wanted to clap my hands in excitement but stopped before I embarrassed myself.

"Yeah. With Harris?" Lenox elaborated.

"Harrison, yes."

Harrison had been at Connor's apartment every day since he was released from the hospital taking care of Connor. I liked Harrison, he was a nice guy. He wanted a commitment, but Connor didn't and kept him on the back burner. Maybe the gunshot to the gut had woken him up and made him realize that life is short. As if either of us needed the reminder; however, Connor seemed to have forgotten how to be happy. I wanted this for him. I wanted him to find someone to love and have a life with.

He deserved it, we both did.

Connor never showed up, he texted and said that he and Harrison were taking a weekend trip and he'd check in later.

The five of us sat outside, ate good food, drank beer – minus Lily, and played poker. We laughed until we cried. It was a good night. And unlike the first time we all sat around the poker table, when the night was done, Jasper took me and Jason home.

CHAPTER TWENTY-THREE

Jasper

I struggled through the last hour of poker. Not because I wasn't having a great time with our friends. I was. We were having a blast. However, all I could think about was Emily perched up on the bathroom counter, me between her legs. The moment Jason said he was tired, I announced we were leaving. That brought about a round of ball busting and name calling.

I didn't give two shits if the guys knew I wanted to get my woman home and all to myself. I also didn't care when Clark said it was nice to finally see me pussy whipped. He could call it whatever he wanted. I was calling it heaven.

When we pulled up to the house, Jason was already asleep in the backseat.

He barely woke up when I carried him in the house and into his room. I set him in bed getting ready to leave so Emily could change him into pajamas when he woke up.

"Jasper?" he asked, his voice full of sleep.

"Right here, bud."

"Do we get to live here forever?" he asked.

I struggled to find an answer that Emily would approve of. I didn't think she'd appreciate the "Fuck yes" that I wanted to say.

So instead I settled on, "That's up to you and your mom."

"Okay." He rolled back to his side.

I gave Emily a kiss on the forehead and left her to do her thing with Jason. I had grown to love that kid. Not because he was Emily's son. But because he was smart and wicked funny. He helped me fix things in the garage and asked a thousand questions about how things worked. He was my buddy, and I loved having him around. I hoped Emily had made up her mind about staying. She still hadn't given me an answer. I was trying to be patient. However, I totally sucked at it.

I moved to the bedroom, closing the door behind me. I pulled my tee, jeans, and boxers off, tossing them in the direction of the hamper. I thought better of the mess I was leaving on the floor and took two steps to pick up the clothes, knowing that Emily would do it if I didn't. She didn't need to be picking up after me. When I opened the lid to the hamper, I saw a pair of red panties on the top of the pile of dirty clothes. I groaned remembering what those looked like against her pale skin. The lace sheer enough to see the hair at the top of her pussy poke through. When I pulled them down her legs, I remembered catching a glimpse of how wet she had been, and I hadn't even touched her yet. Just the promise of my fingers excited her.

I took my hard dick in my hand and gave it a firm tug. I needed to get a shower and take care of this before Emily and I got into bed. I was too worked up and needed some relief so I could take my time with her.

The door opened and Emily walked in. She stood frozen as she closed the door behind her. I felt her gaze on me, warming my skin everywhere she looked. It looked like her hunger matched mine. I was more than ready to take her. It was more than need, it was a compulsion I never knew existed. For once, it wasn't about the sexual release, it was the bond, the connection I desperately wanted. She and I connected in the most intimate way two people can be, not mindless sex, but *mindful* sex. My emotions were fully engaged.

"Starting without me," she purred.

"Thinking about it," I told her.

"Can I help?" She reached behind her and popped the lock on the door.

She sashayed her fine ass over to where I was standing and slid the straps of her dress over her shoulders and let it pool at her feet. The strapless bra that could barely keep her tits contained came off. Next, she let it dangle in her hand for a second before she dropped it. My own sexy striptease. She hooked her fingers on either side of her panties at her hips and pushed them past her thighs until gravity took over and they too were on the floor.

She licked her lips drawing my attention from her chest up to her mouth.

"You are so pretty, Em. You take my breath away."

I sounded like a pansy ass, but I didn't care. She had to know how stunning she was.

"Thank you." She stepped closer and put her hand on my chest. When I reached for her, she stopped me. "It's my turn. For right now, I want to touch you. When your hands are on me, I can't concentrate. And I want this to be good for you."

Was she crazy? It was always good for me.

"I'm all yours." I dropped my hands to my sides and braced for her sensual assault.

Emily didn't waste any time. Scoring her nails down my chest followed by her soft tongue circling one nipple then the other, her hands moved over the ridges of my stomach, my muscles tightening under her expert touch. She licked down the center of my chest down to my belly button, continuing south she kissed her way down my happy trail. She steadied herself with her hands on my thighs and lowered herself to her knees.

I couldn't take my eyes off her as she licked just shy of where I wanted her mouth, down farther completely missing my balls. She moved to the other side and started her slow torturous ascent still not licking where I wanted.

She was killing me. My dick was straining toward her face, yet she ignored it. Instead, she teased me with soft kisses and periodically bit the sensitive skin gently. By the time her hand wrapped around my dick, I was panting. The first swipe of her tongue had me seeing stars, and by the time she had licked her way around the head to the underside I thought I was going to come out of my skin. Was it possible to come from head licking?

She must've lost patience, because with one long wet swipe of her tongue from base to tip, she was done with her tease and took the head of my dick in her mouth sucking with perfect force.

"Holy fuck."

My outburst seemed to fuel her onward; she took more of me into her mouth and cupped my balls, gently massaging them as she continued to flatten her tongue, bathing my dick on her down stroke and sucking on the way up.

Over and over. Up and down she went. She wasn't sucking my dick, she was worshiping it. Never had a blowjob felt so fucking good. Her other hand came up and gripped the base, every time she went up her hand followed. Her tongue continued to swirl on the way down, her hand adding more pressure on what couldn't fit in her mouth.

My hands itched to touch her. I fought back the urge to fist her hair and feel the soft strands pull through my fingers as her head bobbed. Finally, I couldn't hold out any longer. I clenched my ass trying to stop the rush of pleasure.

"I'm gonna come, baby. You need to pull off if you don't want me to come in your mouth," I warned. She doubled her efforts and rolled my balls in her hand. "Oh fuck, Emily. Now."

In a rush of red-hot pleasure, I shot off in an explosion that had my muscles tightening painfully. I was simultaneously desperate for it to end and also continue forever.

She pulled her mouth off of my dick with a pop and sat her ass back on her heels, endless pools of blue desire stared back at me, a wide, satisfied smile pulled at the corner of her sinful mouth. She knew she had rocked my world, and if I was a betting man, I'd bet she was damn proud of herself that I couldn't hold out. Firm tits sat on full display and my mouth watered to taste them. I reached my hand to her to help her up, not allowing her to settle on her feet before I hoisted her up forcing her to wrap her legs around my hips.

"That was fantastic." I leaned in to kiss her, and she pulled her head back.

"You just, you know. You sure you wanna kiss me?"

The thought hadn't crossed my mind. I'd never kissed a woman after she had given me head, but the thought of kissing her after didn't faze me.

"I just what, Em? Came in your mouth? Yeah, I

remember it was fucking otherworldly. I couldn't give two shits if I taste myself on your tongue."

She leaned in, and much like she did with my dick, she did the most amazing things with her tongue in my mouth.

I walked us to the bed and let her top half fall to the mattress, keeping her legs wrapped around me. My eyes traveled her body, and my dick jerked coming back to life. In a rare moment of self-doubt, I lowered myself to hover over her.

"Are you sure you want to do this? We can wait."

CHAPTER TWENTY-FOUR

Emily

What did he just say? Was I sure? Was he out of his ever-loving mind? He was seriously asking me to form a coherent thought when he was naked looming over me with all of his muscles on display. I didn't want to talk. The time for talking was over.

I took advantage of him leaning over me and closed the distance, kissing him again. I loved kissing Jasper. It had become my favorite thing to do – any excuse to feel his lips on mine. The lazy kisses he gave me before he left for work. The aggressive, demanding kisses when he was working us up. The ones that were full of need and lust when he was bringing us down from orgasms. They were all spectacular.

His dick jerked between us, I pulled back from the kiss in surprise. "Already?" I whispered against his lips.

"I told you, you inspire me. Did you not believe me?" he said.

If he was ready, and I was more than ready, what were we waiting for?

"I want you inside me." I licked the seam of his lips, then his neck. He tasted a little salty and a whole lot fucking sexy. I needed him to hurry.

"Not so fast."

His mouth went to my neck, and he sucked and licked his way down to my chest. His hand went between us, his thumb found my wetness and smeared it up to my clit, rubbing hard slow circles that he knew would drive me wild. My hips bucked as he sucked a nipple into his mouth. Sweet Jesus his mouth was wicked.

"Please," I begged. My hands fisted the comforter harder, and I lifted my hips to reiterate I was ready.

He reached over to the bedside table and opened the drawer pulling out an unopened box of condoms. I don't know why that made me feel better that the box was brand new and he'd never used any from the package, but the petty, jealous girl in me did.

He pulled one out and tossed the box on the table. With the corner of the wrapper in his mouth, he opened the foil and spit the piece in his mouth off to the side. He reached down and grabbed his dick in one hand and rolled the condom down his long shaft.

"Scoot back, all the way on the bed," he instructed.

I quickly did as he asked. He planted his knee on the bed and crawled over me, leaving me mesmerized by the way his muscles flexed and moved. When he settled between my spread legs, he came down on one elbow as he brushed my hair off my shoulder and placed a soft peck there before moving to my neck.

He pushed his hips forward, his dick rubbing between my legs, the head bumping my clit. The friction of his movement was driving me mad. I wiggled my hips trying to get him where I really wanted him. Finally, he reached between us and in one long slow glide he pushed inside of me.

My back arched and I threw my head back. "Oh God." My skin felt like it was on fire, every part of me heating up. He pulled back just as slowly as he'd pushed in, leaving just the tip in before he thrust forward giving me his full length. With two strokes, he had pushed me past all rational thought, and hormones took over.

"Baby, please move," I pleaded.

"Not yet. I don't want to hurt you."

"Now, Jasper. I need you to fuck me now."

That did it. With both elbows planted on either side of my head, he fisted my hair. He pulled back and drove forward with such force he moved us farther up the bed. I hooked my ankles and squeezed my thighs together and matched him thrust for thrust. I threaded my fingers with his on top of my head, just wanting to hold his hand as he picked up his pace.

His face came up from my neck and found my lips. His kiss was in complete contradiction to the way he pounded into me – it was soft and sensual. A lover's kiss. The juxtaposition of sensations was spurring me closer to climax. He had said he was gonna fuck me senseless, and he was right. I couldn't think, I could barely breathe. He slowed his pace, changing the rhythm hitting the spot deep inside of me, a spot I didn't even knew existed.

"Slow it down, Em," he said.

"I can't," I panted.

"You can, baby. I wanna go with you." He rocked harder, not helping his cause.

I couldn't stop the wave that was building even if I had tried. He was rubbing some special magic button inside of me, and his pubic bone was scraping against my clit on every down stroke. Everything was escalating so fast, and just when I thought the dam was going to break and I was going to fall over the edge, nothing happened. The feeling kept building.

"Oh God," I moaned pushing my head harder against the bed. Jasper didn't waste any time licking my now exposed throat and kissing my chin. "What's happening?"

Something was happening, something big, something I wasn't sure I wanted to happen. Everything was sensitized, I could feel every fine hair on my body standing on end.

"Almost there," he groaned. "Let go."

I shook my head trying to stop whatever was happening, but it wouldn't stop.

"Oh fuck."

"That's it, baby. Fuck, Emily."

When it broke it wasn't a dam, it was a geyser that shot me out of this universe somewhere far, far away. My vision blurred, and before I could let out a wail of pure unadulterated bliss, Jasper took my mouth and silenced me. He slowed his strokes to lazy, gentle glides, bringing us both down to earth.

My breathing returned to normal, and somewhere in the throes of ecstasy, I must've closed my eyes because when I opened them Jasper's handsome face was gentled and he was looking down at me.

"Hey," he whispered.

"Hi." I smiled.

He brushed my sweaty hair off my face, his thumb brushing my cheek. "Welcome back." He returned the smile.

"What was that?" I asked.

Jasper chuckled and kissed my forehead. "Let me get rid of this." He pulled out and went to go throw the condom away.

I rolled to my side to pull the covers down and climbed in. Jasper might have no issues walking around naked with his cut muscles and perfect body, but I preferred not to be lying naked when he got back.

What the fuck was that? I sat up and felt the bed, it was soaked like I had peed the bed. I was patting the comforter when Jasper came back into the bedroom.

"What are you doing?" he asked noting my frantic movement.

"Nothing?" It was meant to be an answer, but it sounded more like a question even to my own ears.

Jasper moved to the bed, and when he saw where I was feeling, he looked up at me with a smug grin gracing his face. I thought I was going to die of embarrassment. I didn't know what to say, or how to ask. But this was ridiculous. Could a woman even pee when she was having sex? Because I think I peed the bed.

"Why's the bed so wet?" I asked my face heating up to five hundred degrees.

He didn't answer right away, he pulled back the covers, slid into bed, and once he was settled, he tagged me by my arm and pulled me to him. He tucked me in close and started to graze my back with his fingertips.

"Why's the bed so wet?" he repeated then answered, "That's all you."

"All me?" I asked. "I don't mean to sound like an ass, but I've had sex before, and the bed has never been that wet."

"Good. Well, good for me, bad for you I guess."

"What does that mean?"

"I'm happy that I'm the only man that has ever made you orgasm so intense that you left the bed that wet. Bad for you, because if that felt half as good for you as it did for me, then baby, you've been missing out."

"You got that right," I mumbled. "I didn't know."

Oh God. I was really talking about this with him.

We had just had sex. Mind-blowingly good sex, earth-shattering, in fact. And here I was asking why the bed was wet. What the hell was wrong with me?

"Know what?" he prompted.

"I've changed my mind about asking questions. I'll Google it. We should just lie here and let me relax in my post best-sex-ever buzz."

"I gotta tell you, I'm pleased as fuck that you're buzzing with post best-sex-ever high. But there's nothing we can't talk about. There's never a reason to be ashamed or embarrassed in our bed."

"Okay."

"And one more thing you should know. That was hands down best-sex-ever for me, too. And not just physically, emotionally, too. There might not have been anything sweet and gentle in the movements, but I felt every part of our connection to my soul."

I started to drift off, the hand rubbing my back lulling me to sleep. I should've put some clothes on in case Jason needed me, but I didn't want to lose the skin-on-skin contact. We molded together perfectly.

CHAPTER TWENTY-FIVE

Jasper

"I'm not drinking that fruity girly shit. If I wanted a juice box, I'd take one of Jason's Capri Suns," I told Harrison when he offered me a try of his Blue Hawaiian.

We were all at our favorite restaurant, great burgers and the coldest draft craft beer in the entire state. It wasn't too long ago it was just the four of us. Me, Lenox, Clark, and Levi would come in here when we got home from a mission and enjoy a meal. Nothing screamed the good 'ole US of A like a burger and beer. Now our tribe has grown. Lenox had Lily and Carter. I had Emily and Jason, and somehow Connor and Harrison came with them like a package deal or some shit. Over the last two months, Connor and I had formed a pretty tight friendship. He kind of slid into the group and fit in. Harrison was growing on me, a little. His saving grace was that he was good to Jason. Connor's job had taken him away a few times, but unlike mine, he didn't leave the country.

It seemed that the assholes of the world had taken a break from being assholes and the team hadn't been deployed in over three months. I was starting to get a little restless. I was used to the rush of my job, I loved it. Even though Emily and Jason were waiting at home for me every day when I got off work, my job had become boring. It wasn't in my DNA to be a desk jockey. The only good part was I did get to spend a lot of time with them.

Emily's laugh pulled me from my musings. "Could you imagine Jasper drinking a fruity vodka drink?"

"It's rum," Harrison corrected looking a little dejected that I wouldn't try his drink.

"Hand it over," Clark said. "Unlike these pretty boys, I'm secure in my manhood."

The table laughed.

"What the hell does not liking fruit juice with my alcohol have to do with my manhood?" I asked.

"Nothing, I suppose. I just wanted to question

your manhood now that Emily has your balls in a sling," Clark said. I shot him a look over the table and glanced at Jason. "Oops. Sorry."

"Mama, did you take Jasper's slingshot away, too? Uncle Connor bought me one, but Mom said I couldn't have it, that I would shoot out the windows," Jason explained.

Lily lost the battle, her water spraying out of her mouth onto the table in front of her. She quickly grabbed a napkin off the table to wipe her face. "Yeah, Jasper. Did Emily take your slingshot?" Lily giggled.

There was so much I could say about what Emily did with my balls and how fucking great she was at it. Unfortunately, with Jason sitting there, those thoughts died in my head.

"Bud, there comes a time in a man's life when he meets a woman. Not just any woman, but the perfect woman. When he meets her, she complements him in every way. Now, when that woman comes along, a smart man, he knows that she's one-of-a-kind and gladly hands his slingshot over. A man will always choose his woman over a toy."

"I get to keep *my* toys, right? No way, I'm giving away my Legos," Jason asked.

"Your Legos are safe."

"Can I get you anything else?" The waitress walked over to the table standing next to me. She was making me uncomfortable standing way too close. I put my arm around Emily and pulled her a little closer. "Not for me. Babe, you want anything else?"

"No, thank you." Emily smiled and shook her head. She'd caught on to what I was doing.

"I think we're good."

The waitress looked at my arm around Emily then back at me and walked away.

"You always get hit on like that?" Emily asked.

"Everywhere," Clark helpfully answered.

"No. He's exaggerating." I shook my head telling Clark this was not up for discussion. Emily knew about my past. I wasn't going to allow her face to get rubbed in my stupidity. If she wanted to know something, I would tell her. Not my friends, and not at a table where she could be embarrassed or hurt. I didn't like thinking about all the women I had been with, so I knew she sure as fuck didn't want to hear about them.

"So, Shane and I have something to tell you all," Lily started. Lenox threw his arm around his wife's shoulder and smiled. "We're gonna have another baby."

Congratulations came out of my mouth, and a

smile hit my face. Fist bumps were exchanged, and Emily got up to hug Lily. I had become a master of masking my emotions, this moment was no different. I pretended to be happy for my friends and toasted their good news. But inside? Inside my gut twisted and panic bubbled to the surface. Lily had almost died when she was delivering baby Carter. What did I do? I didn't stay and support my friends. My pussy ass ran. I couldn't see past my grief to stand by my friend while his wife and child were in distress. All I could think about was Liz dying.

Seeing Lily pregnant the first time around was torture. I'd always thought that when the two rabbits decided to get pregnant again, I'd ask the Commander to put me out in the field. A nine-month field assignment so I didn't have to see Lily start to show and see the excitement on their faces. I was a coward and a complete dick. Now that I had Emily, I couldn't run to the Middle East somewhere and hide out. Fuck.

The conversation flowed around me, and I listened. Emily sensing my mood change had gotten closer, her hand on my leg that was normally soothing did nothing.

"I hate to cut this short, but I'm exhausted," Emily announced.

"Yeah, it's getting pretty late. I need to get Carter down," Lily agreed.

We said our goodbyes, more hugs and congratulations were said.

By the time we'd gotten home, I had needed a minute alone. Emily didn't say a word when we walked in the house, and she took Jason to help him get ready for bed.

I grabbed a beer and went out to the back deck. I sat out there long after I finished my beer, lost in thought. Why hadn't Emily given me an answer yet if she and Jason would move in? They were still living with me, but when she spoke to her mother, who incidentally was batshit crazy, Emily always said they were *staying* here. Not *living* here. She hadn't told her mom that she was looking for places to move to, nor had she brought it up to me. But she had yet to make it official. I checked my watch, and it was well past eleven, I'd been out on the deck for hours.

I tossed my bottle in the trash, locked up the house, and checked in on Jason. He was sound asleep in his bed. Exactly where he should be. As fucked up as my head was, one thing was certain. I loved Emily and Jason. I couldn't imagine my life without them.

When I entered our bedroom, Emily was already

in bed. Her back was to me, and she was under a mountain of covers. That woman was always cold until I warmed her up then all the covers ended up on the floor. I undressed and got into bed behind her, her sexy ass pushed against my dick as she tried to cuddle closer.

I kissed the back of her head and tucked her in. Her ass wiggled again, and my dick jumped to life.

"Babe," I warned.

She pushed her ass back and turned her head looking over her shoulder at me. "I need you," she whispered.

I didn't deserve this woman. Even after I had been silent and distant on the way home she was still giving, not only of her body but her support.

I ran my hands over her belly down between her legs, spreading her folds, checking her readiness. She was wet and slippery and fucking hot.

I guided myself to her opening and slid inside. Home.

"I love you, Emily," I whispered into her hair gently rocking into her massaging her breast with my free hand.

There was no urgency for release tonight. Our lovemaking was slow and gentle, a perfect coupling. I kept a lazy rhythmic pace wanting it to last as long as possible. Emily was nearing her breaking point. Her back arched and her hips moved countering my strokes, her movements detonating my release. My balls tightened, and my dick stiffened even more. Her orgasm broke, and her pussy convulsed. I planted myself deep and let go with her, the pulsations in her pussy drawing my orgasm out.

With my arm wrapped tightly around her and my dick still deep, I drifted to sleep.

CHAPTER TWENTY-SIX

Emily

Thank God it was Saturday, and I didn't have to get up to take Jason to school. Jasper wasn't in bed with me when I woke up this morning. I rolled to my back and stared up at the ceiling. What was I doing? It had been over three months since I had worked. I hadn't even been seriously looking for a job. Years ago I had taken some classes in graphic design but never finished my degree. Over the years I'd kept up with the latest design software and had taught myself everything I didn't learn when I stopped going to school. My logos and designs were pretty damn good. I started selling my pre-made work online and had picked up a few custom orders. Nothing huge, but I had some spending money. Jasper refused to take money for rent or food, so we were basically living here for free. I argued with him about letting me pay, especially after everything he had purchased for the house. He explained that all the things I did around the house more than paid for rent. I didn't believe him, but it did feel good he appreciated me cleaning and cooking. I enjoyed taking care of him and Jason. I loved him coming home every day to us.

There had been some changes in Jasper over the last few weeks, little things. I figured he was getting antsy about not getting deployed. I mentioned it to Lily, and she confirmed Lenox was the same way. It made sense; the guys were always on the go. And recently, they'd been doing nothing but training. Plus side for me was Jasper's already impressive muscles had gotten even bigger and harder. Last night, after Lily announced she was pregnant, had been the biggest change. He thought he hid it, that when his mask came down none of us could see through it. We could. I could. I knew that man like the back of my hand, his every mood.

He was freaked the hell out that she was pregnant. And I didn't know how to help him. Well, I did know how to help, however, not without possibly destroying our relationship. I was trying to find a way to broach the subject with Jasper when he walked in the bedroom.

"Morning, beautiful," he said on a smile.

He was so damn good-looking and sweet. Which sounded ridiculous describing a badass as sweet, but he was. He was thoughtful, kind, generous, supportive – everything I could ever want in a man was wrapped up in Jasper.

That's why this was going to suck. Possibly shatter my soul. But I had to do it. Not for me or Jason, but for him.

"Morning," I replied. "I should get up and get Jason ready."

Connor would be here soon to pick Jason up. He was taking him to Savannah for the weekend. It was the perfect time to talk to Jasper in case we both had melt-downs so Jason wouldn't be here to see it.

"Connor already picked him up."

Holy crap. "I didn't realize it was so late. He wasn't packed." I started to get out of bed as if I could do something now that they were gone.

"Slow down. Connor was early. He said he wanted to beat the weekend traffic. I packed Jason up."

See! Thoughtful and kind.

"Sorry," I grumbled. I couldn't believe I didn't even kiss my boy good-bye before they left.

"Don't be. It wasn't a problem. Connor will have Jason Facetime you when they get to the hotel. You hungry?"

Even though my stomach was empty, my nerves wouldn't allow me to eat.

"No, but thank you."

"What's wrong?" he asked his eyes narrowing.

I should've known I wouldn't have been able to hide anything from him. This was why I lost at poker every time we played with the guys; I was incapable of hiding my emotions.

"Let me get dressed." I felt too vulnerable talking to him while I was still in bed naked.

I thought he was going to demand I tell him, but instead, he said, "I'll wait for you in the living room."

I waited for him to leave before I jumped out of bed and got dressed. I brushed my hair and debated whether or not to pull it up. Jasper loved my hair down, he told me often how beautiful it was, how much he loved to run his fingers through it. I decided against the ponytail, I needed to use everything I had in my arsenal to remind him that he cared for me. If that meant something as silly as my hair, I'd use it. Stupid? Yes. Completely irrational, yes. Yet there I was trying it.

Jasper was on the couch flipping through the sports channels when I joined him. He immediately turned the TV off and tossed the remote on the table.

"What's going on?" he asked. No small talk, straight to the point. "Whatever it is I can fix it."

"I hope so," I grumbled. "We need to talk about Lily."

"What about Lily?"

"Actually, more to the point your reaction to her being pregnant," I said.

There it was – his mouth got tight, there was a shift in the air, and the mask came down. "That reaction." I pointed out.

"I'm happy for them," he said not acknowledging the problem.

"I know you are. But that doesn't negate the wall you just threw up."

"I didn't put up a wall between us," he argued.

"Jasper, you have never lied to me. Don't start now. You might not be intentionally building it between you and me, but baby, you just built a fortress around yourself. And I'm afraid you're gonna lock yourself in there."

Jasper's expression was as hard as the very stones in the wall I accused him of building. Hard like granite. Unbreakable.

"You think I'm lying to you? What the fuck, Emily?" Jasper stood and starting walking the room.

This was exactly what I was afraid of. He was not ready to hear what I had to say.

"No. I think you're lying to yourself. Before we started this, you told me you had to tell me something. When you started that conversation, you asked me not to interrupt you. I'm asking you now to let me talk and you listen." He nodded his head, and I continued. "It's time you deal with your feelings surrounding Liz and Alesha. I know you looked into their medical records, you read the files, but nowhere in that conversation did you tell me that you called Liz's family to speak to them personally or had you gone back to Montana to make things right with Liz."

"How the fuck would I make things right with Liz? She's dead, remember? She died, alone, delivering my dead baby because I was too busy fucking the memory of her out of my head."

Ouch. I really didn't want to hear that, but he was proving my point.

"How'd that work out for you?" I asked. "Did it work? Did fucking any of those women make you forget Liz or Alesha? Did any of them make you feel better? God knows there were thousands, Jasper. At any point did any of them look past your dick and into your soul and magically reach in and pull the memory of your daughter from your head?"

"Not until you. Not until I met you, and for the first time since they died I felt something, a moment of peace where I didn't remember them."

Jesus Christ that was the best and the worst thing I had ever heard in my life.

"I want you to find peace in our love. I want to be the one who soothes the broken pieces. I want to be the one who helps you heal, not forget. You need to remember them. I want to remember them. They are a part of you, your history. I love them because I love all of you. The good and the bad. You have to forgive yourself. You'll never be ready to make promises to me, to us, if you don't. We'll never be able to have a future, a family, children of our own until you forgive yourself."

"You want more kids?" His face paled.

"Yes, and I want them with you. Jasper, I will help you. I will stand by you every step. But, you have to start, take the first step in forgiving yourself, and I promise you I will hold us together the rest of the way."

"I have to go," he said.

My heart dropped to the floor precariously teetering on the edge of the cliff. One wrong move and it would be shattered forever.

The door slammed behind him.

CHAPTER TWENTY-SEVEN

Jasper

"Shane thought you might be here," Lily's voice stopped my next punch from landing on the bag still swinging in front of me.

My anger spiked then I remembered she was pregnant. "Everything alright?" I turned to look at her.

"No."

"Where's Lenox? Is the baby okay?" I stalked to her. Was she crazy? Why was she all the way out here?

"Shane's in the car with Carter. I asked to come in first," she explained.

"Why?"

"To tell you this," she started. "When you and

the guys came to get me when I ran from Shane you told me something. I've never forgotten your words. While you're trying to figure out whatever is going on in your head, I want you to remember what you said to me: *When two people are destined to be together and share the love that you two have, there is no getting over the other person.* You have to ask yourself, do you and Emily share that same love? The same kind of love that you told me I'd never get over in a thousand lifetimes. If you do, you better hold on with both hands because I'm telling you what's on the other side of this is worth it."

"You don't understand." What the fuck. This wasn't about whether I wanted to be with Emily. I loved her.

"I do understand. I understand that you are getting ready to throw something beautiful away because you refuse to let the shadows that still clouds your vision go. I love you, Jasper. I have never pried or pushed you to talk. But you have to know it hurts me to see you in pain and not let anyone in. And just because you told the guys what happened, doesn't mean you've let them in. It just means you told them a sad story."

After that gut check, Lily didn't wait for my response. She turned on her heel and walked out of the shed. I started back to my punching bag when the door opened again. Jesus Christ, was I Ebenezer Scrooge and being visited by my past, present, and future? That was impossible. My past was dead, and my future was fucked.

"You gotta minute?" Oh, good it was Clark. He was the less touchy-feely of the guys. He hated messes that included things like feelings and emotions. He avoided those topics like the plague.

"Whatcha got?" I asked.

"For fuck sakes, get a towel, your knuckles are dripping blood all over the concrete."

I looked down at my hands not even realizing they were bleeding. I hadn't bothered with gloves; I welcomed the pain of my bare fist slamming into the black vinyl. I cleaned my knuckles and sat in the desk chair opposite of him.

Clark took a minute to gather his thoughts before he began. "I don't like to pry into others' personal shit. I figured when you were ready, you'd share more. But you haven't."

"Nothing more to share. I told you all the whole story."

"Wrong answer. You shared what happened, not what you're still going through. Which I gotta tell you is insulting. You think none of us notice you're hurting, but all of us wanted to give you privacy."

"Seriously? Since when have any of us opened up about feelings? Especially you. You're wired tight, brother," I reminded him.

"True. However, I know that if my shit got to be too much, you'd all have my back. So far, I've been able to carry my burden. You, not so much. I suspect it's because while my shit is painful, it doesn't compare to losing a child the way you did." When I remained silent, he shook his head and continued. "I know a little about the guilt you're carrying around. You know the last thing I said to my little brother before he died?"

"No."

Clark never talked about his brother. He was killed when the transport helo he was in was shot down by an RPG.

"*I wish you were dead.* That was after I caught him in bed with my wife and kicked his ass. He left for his deployment a few weeks later." I had no idea Clark had been married. "I know the regret of doing and saying something and never getting the chance to make it right. I live with the fact my brother died knowing I wanted him to die. And in that fit of rage, I might've wanted to kill him. But I didn't, and as pissed as I was he was fucking my wife, I still loved him. I left that night and never looked back."

"Fuck man, I had no idea. I don't know what to say."

"Nothing to say. I told you that fucked up family drama so I could tell you this. I had to forgive myself. The weight of that guilt was crushing. It affected all aspects of my life. It's time for you to let it go, too. You're gonna lose Emily if you don't."

"How do you know that? Did you talk to her?" I asked.

"Didn't have to talk to her, man, that woman for reasons only known to her loves you. Unlike all the other bar skanks you've screwed over the years, she sees you. Not your uniform, or your wallet, and not your dick. She wants you. You can't give her that unless you fix yourself. I'd bet my next re-up bonus she'll wait for you if you ask her to. But if you wait and fuck around, she'll find someone who's willing to put in the work and give her a family. Christ, you freaked out last night when Lily told us she was pregnant. How are you gonna give that woman babies when you can't even see Lily pregnant?"

"I don't want kids."

"Bullshit. Go blow smoke up someone else's ass. I see you with Jason. You adore that kid."

"I do. He's a cool kid." Clark sat quietly and waited me out, I couldn't bullshit him. "I bailed on Liz, like a scared boy. And I just did it to Emily. She asked me to forgive myself, even promised me she'd help. And what did I do? I fucking ran. How the hell can I be a father when I can't even be the man my woman needs?"

"I can't answer that. Only you can. I can tell you this, you and I? We've been in some tight spots together, unfriendlies all around, pinned down, and when I thought all hope of getting out alive was gone, there was you, taking my six and pulling us through. It's in you, you just can't see it through your guilt." Clark stood and picked his phone up off the desk. "Sort your shit. Do what you do best, tighten the kill chain."

"Find, track, fix, and kill," I said.

"You've found the problem, now track it, fix it, and kill that shit, so it never comes back to haunt you."

Long after he was gone, I sat at my desk thinking about everything Emily, Lily, and Clark had said. The answer to my problem was simple – the execution not so much.

I made a few phone calls and sent a text to Emily.

I'm not running. I need a few days.

Her response came quick.

Okay. I'll go stay at Lily's.

The hell she would.

Please stay at the house. I need to know that you are sleeping in our bed.

There still wasn't a response by the time I had locked up the shed and got in my car. I was about to abandon my plan and go directly to her when my phone vibrated.

Okay.

I drove to the airport and parked in the long-term parking. I hadn't bothered purchasing a ticket in advance. It was going to cost a mint either way. After trying two airlines, I finally found one with a direct flight to Montana leaving within the hour. By the time I made it through security and to the gate, the flight was boarding.

It was time to face what I'd done.

***

LIZ'S SISTER wasn't hard to track down. I debated going to see her parents as soon as I landed, but I had to make things right with Reagan first.

I knocked on the door, and I was a little taken

aback when a man answered. "Is Reagan here?" I asked.

"Yeah, can I tell her who's here?" he asked.

I thought about telling him to tell her douchebag was here, but I opted for my name instead. He closed the door behind him, and moments later Reagan appeared in front of me. A little apprehensive but oddly enough not surprised. Which was crazy because I was shocked I was standing in front of her.

"I wondered how long it would take you to come," she said. "Come in." She opened the door wide and stepped aside.

If I was overseas I would think this was some sort of ambush; no way should she be inviting me into her home. I had to remind myself that this was Liz's sister inviting me in, not some Jihadi terrorist. I was actually surprised she didn't tell me to fuck off and slam the door in my face

"Nice place you have here," I said for a lack of anything else to say.

"You didn't come all this way to talk about my house, Jasper."

"No. I came here to apologize. Only, on the way over here, I realized that there's nothing I can say to make things right. I abandoned your sister, my friend, and my child. That makes me the lowest form of shit. However, I wanted you to know, when I called Liz I was calling to tell her I was on my way. Way too late, I know."

I waited for her to kick me out, or scream at me, hell I was waiting for the man that answered the door to come in the room and try to kick my ass. I wouldn't have blamed them if they had.

"You know, Eliza would be really pissed at me if she was alive for me telling you to go to hell. She always said that in another life, the two of you would sail off into the sunset together. You know Liz, always the dreamer." I smiled and remembered the way Liz always looked at everything through rose-tinted glasses. She believed in fairy tales. "She knew that you had a different calling and was proud of you for following your heart. And don't worry that she wasn't pining away for you, she just had a special soft spot for you."

I knew Liz did, and I had one for her. We were each other's firsts in high school. That was another reason this was so hard. Liz had been there for all the important things in my life through high school, and after we split, we were still just as close. I knew about every boyfriend she had. She told me everything.

"Anyway, I'm sorry for what I said to you. I was hurting badly. Losing Alesha and Liz the same day the way we did, I wasn't thinking. I should've told you what happened. Despite what went on between the two of you, you had a right to know. I have some stuff for you."

Reagan broke down and started crying and sat on the couch. I sat next to her and pulled her in for a hug.

"I'm so sorry, Rea. I'll never forgive myself."

How could I let go of my guilt when my actions caused so much grief to Liz's family? I deserved to carry it around with me for the rest of my life. Emily and Jason were better off with a man that was whole and could take care of them. It was better she found out now before she wasted any more time with me.

"She wrote to you, Liz did. She kept a journal. She knew that you'd come around, and when you did, you'd want to know everything you'd missed. So she wrote everything down for you so she wouldn't forget. I'm sorry I read the journal. I know it was wrong, but I missed her so much I needed to have a part of her, even if it was just seeing her handwriting. Hold on."

Reagan stood and jogged to the back of the house before I could stop her. When she came back with a red leather-bound book, I put my hand up to stop her.

"I don't deserve that. You should keep it, Rea."

"How long have I known you?" she asked.

That was an odd question. "I don't know the exact years. But a long time."

"Long enough to know that you've been beating yourself up for the last four years. You made a mistake, and you were a dick. But that mistake did not kill my sister or Alesha. Even if you had been with Liz, she'd still be dead. What happened was horrible, but no one's fault."

"I might not have been able to prevent it, but I still abandoned her. And she died alone and scared."

"No, she didn't. Is that what you've thought?" I nodded my head and closed my eyes pulling up the scene in the hospital the way I'd imagined it to be. "She wasn't alone. Alesha hadn't moved in a few hours. She called her doctor, he said to drink some orange juice and lie down. She did, an hour later the baby still hadn't moved. When she called her doctor back, he told her to go to the hospital and go to labor and delivery and he'd meet her there. I picked her up and took her. We were planning on going shopping after." Reagan took a deep breath before she finished her story. "There was no heartbeat. An ultrasound machine was brought in and confirmed that Alesha was gone. My parents came to the hospital, and it took hours for us to calm her down before she'd let the doctor start to induce her labor. Alesha was delivered, and Liz went into cardiac arrest, and her lungs stopped working. The doctors tried everything to save her. And I know you won't believe this." Reagan had to stop again to regain her composure. "But it's almost like she gave up. She couldn't bear to live without Alesha and didn't fight to stay here with us."

I believed that Reagan thought that Liz let go to be with Alesha, and I wasn't going to offer her my thoughts. If Reagan needed that to make things easier, who was I to question her?

"Thank you for being with her when I wasn't. That will always be my biggest regret."

"Don't let one regret ruin your life. You deserve to be happy. One bad choice shouldn't define the rest of your life. You know my sister would hate that for you. You have to forgive yourself so you can move on."

"I've already heard that more than once today," I mumbled.

"Really? Is that why you're here?" she asked.

I told Reagan the story. First how I met Emily and how I behaved when I found out she had a child, to the robbery, all the way through today. I told her about Lily and Lenox and how I left the hospital when their child was born. What I did leave out of the story was how I'd whored around all these years. I sounded like a big enough douche already.

"Wow. You really love her, don't you?" Reagan smiled.

I was a little uncomfortable talking about loving Emily with Liz's sister, but she deserved the truth. "More than anything. She's everything. She brightens every part of my dark soul. And Jason, that boy is something else. You know at six he can help me take apart a carburetor and clean it. The boy loves to build..." Reagan had tears streaming down her cheeks. "I'm sorry. I shouldn't have said anything."

"No, no, these are happy tears. I'm happy for you. You should be happy living your life."

"How can you want that for me? How can you forgive me after everything I did to Liz?"

"There's nothing for me to forgive. And Liz already forgave you, a long time ago. You need to read her journal. You'll understand."

"Let me get you one more thing." Reagan disappeared back down the hall, and I was in a daze. Why was she letting me off the hook? She should be pissed and raging, hitting me, anything. Instead, she was compassionate and kind. "You should have this." Reagan held out a shoe box.

"Don't open it here. Wait until you're ready. But they belong to you." I stood to take the box from her. "One more thing before you go. Well, two. Forgive yourself and move on with Emily. Don't let her go. And now that all of this is, I don't know, out in the open, can we please keep in touch? I didn't just lose Liz and Alesha. I lost you, too. Maybe we both needed time to heal, but I miss my Taco Tuesday texts. I have missed *you*."

I threw my head back and belted out a laugh. I couldn't believe that Reagan remembered the Taco Tuesday texts. While everyone was sending around "hump day" texts, me, Liz, and Reagan exchanged Taco Tuesday. It wasn't every Tuesday or very often but enough to make you laugh when out of the blue you'd get a Tuesday message.

"I missed you, too. There are some things I need to work out before I go home to Emily. She deserves me to be whole when I go to her."

"Are you staying in town long?"

"No. I have a few stops then I thought I'd go by and see your parents," I told her.

"No dice, friend. They got the hell out of here and moved to Florida. Dad retired. And Mom said there was no way she was sitting in the house with him all winter with nothing to do. Dad plays golf three times a week, and Mom gardens and paints. Well, she calls it painting, but it's those paint by number things." Reagan chuckled.

"No shit? Good for them. I had no idea they moved. You didn't want to go?" I asked.

"As soon as I finish up this semester, I'm headed down there. My ass is tired of being cold, too."

"That guy who answered? He your boyfriend?" I asked.

"Fred? Yes, that's his name, Fred. Hell no he's not my boyfriend. When Mom and Dad left and I moved out on my own, I felt better with a guy for a roommate. He's kinda a jerk, but at least I feel safe when he's home."

"What do you mean jerk? To you?" I all but growled. Maybe the kid needed a lesson in manners before I left.

"Whoa there, Captain America. Not to me. Just in general. He barely talks to me. He goes to class, work, eats here, sleeps here, and leaves. He's a great roommate in that sense."

We exchanged numbers and promised to stay in touch. It wasn't until I was in the rental car I thought about whether Emily would be okay with me being friends with Liz's sister. If she didn't like it, I'd have to explain to Reagan why I couldn't keep in touch. She'd understand.

I was stalling. I knew I was, since I was driving the speed limit. I might've also circled the block twice. The entrance was coming up again, and before I could puss out, I turned right into the long driveway. I parked, grabbed Liz's journal, and started walking.

When I found the spot I was looking for, I sat down in the grass and stared at the black granite headstone.

Eliza Renea Simmons. Next to her was a headstone with a heart and angel etched into the stone. *Alesha Reagan Walker.*

I had no idea that Liz had planned to give Alesha my last name. I was happy yet felt very undeserving. Alesha was Liz's; she had carried her and nurtured her. I'd done nothing for them, nothing for Alesha. I didn't deserve the honor of Alesha having my last name.

I opened Liz's journal and began to read:

Jasper,

It has been a few weeks since we've spoken. Boy, that didn't go as planned, and for that, I am sorry. I was so caught up in my own fear, I forgot about yours. I need you to understand that while this baby is unexpected, it is not unwanted. My fear does not equal indecision. I know now that I went about telling you about the baby all wrong. In my haste, I blurted out something that should've been handled with care. I haven't called you back, not out of stubbornness or anger but because I know you. I know the boy you were and the man you have become. I know that you need time to process and you'll come to us when you are ready. We both said some pretty hateful things to each other. I also know that neither of us meant a word we said. If there is one thing I am sure of that is, we share a deep friendship that is rooted in respect for one another. Our friendship will survive this.

There is one thing I said that I regret most. I told you I was disappointed in you. That is not the truth. I could never be disappointed in you. While our lives have taken us on different paths to different parts of the world, one thing has always remained true: how proud I am to call you my friend. You are loyal, brave, and trustworthy.

When the time is right, and you are ready, we will work through this together — as friends. Just because we are not married or even a couple doesn't mean that we cannot love our child and parent him or her *together. This child is as much yours as it is mine, and we will love it and share in all the joys together.*

Always,

-Liz

P.S.

I am starting this journal for you. I will keep track of all my doctor visits and milestones so you won't miss a moment of the baby growing. Consider this your first entry – morning sickness does not only happen in the mornings. It is morning, noon, and night sickness. This baby must be a boy and is already taking after the Walkers and proving to be difficult. (You know I'm right.) I will be glad when this part is over.

I closed the book and looked up at the gravestones.

"I'm so sorry, Lizzy. I should've been there for you. I shouldn't have waited so long to call you. So many *should haves*. There are so many things I regret. I hope you knew how much your friendship meant to me. I hope you truly believed the words you wrote. I know we would've been good parents. I hope you forgave me. God, I wish you and Alesha were here. I wanted her, too, Lizzy. I promise you, I wanted her just as much as you did. I have to go." I stood looking at both headstones. "I love you both."

CHAPTER TWENTY-EIGHT

Emily

There was a knock on the door, and my heart slammed into my chest, then I remembered Jasper wouldn't be knocking on his own door. I hadn't heard anything from him since his last text message.

I checked the peephole and smiled.

"What are you doing here?" I asked.

"Oh, nothin'. Just thought I'd come see a friend." Lily held up a bottle of wine.

I stepped aside and let her enter. "Right. Because pregnant women often drive around with bottles of wine in their cars."

"Fine. I thought you could use some company with Jason gone."

"And Jasper."

"Jesus girl. Can't you play along? Fine. I was worried about you with Jason being with Connor and Jasper not here. I'm not being nosey. We can sit and watch a movie while you drink."

"Come on, let's sit. How are you feeling?"

I really didn't want to think about Jasper or what he was doing. He said he wasn't running, he just needed time. Only, he didn't tell me how much time.

"Better now that I'm out of the pukey stage. I was like this with Carter, too."

"Was Lenox gone a lot while you were pregnant with Carter?" I asked.

I couldn't imagine having to go through pregnancy alone. I was lucky, and Steven wasn't on deployment rotation until Jason was nine months old. His help was a godsend.

"Well, that's a long story. I guess now that you know the truth I'm allowed to tell you. I'm sorry I lied to you all those times when Shane was gone. I hope you understand," Lily said, her pretty face scrunched up.

"No need to apologize. I understand. Can you believe I actually thought that they worked checking in gear? Oh my God. Now that I know the truth it's so obvious what they do." I laughed.

"I've known Shane practically my whole life..."

Lily told me the entire story of how Shane Owings became Carter Lenox after faking his death. She explained that for twelve years on the anniversary of his death she would visit his grave. Her and Shane's past was a crazy heart-breaking story. However, in the end, they found their way back to each other and were stronger for it. What I couldn't believe was how strong and brave my friend was. I thought I had a rough few days with Liam and a bank robbery. She had witnessed multiple people being killed, including the man who had kidnapped her and held her at gunpoint. By the time she was done, I was stunned.

"As long as we're sharing, I should tell you the truth about me and Steven." And I went about telling her the whole sordid story.

"Wow," Lily whispered.

"Who knew we were both hiding secrets so big?" I laughed.

"Got any more juicy secrets to tell me?" Lily asked.

By the time midnight had rolled around, I had polished off half a bottle of wine, spilled every secret I had, and laughed until I had cried. It was a great night. After the day I'd had, I needed it. I was scared to death I had gone too far and pushed Jasper away. I knew it was a risk, but one that had to be taken. If I wanted any chance at all to have a future with Jasper, he had to face what happened to Liz and Alesha. I didn't want to be his crutch, I wanted to be his partner. What bothered me was he said I made him forget. That meant that he was sweeping it further under the rug. I had to think about Jason, too. He was already attached to Jasper and would be hurt if things didn't work out.

"Thank you for coming over." I hugged Lily at the front door. "So am I allowed to call Lenox *Shane* now? Shane fits him way better than Lenox anyway."

Lily laughed. "That would be hysterical. Next poker night, you totally should."

"Drive safe. Text me when you get home, please."

"Will do." I watched as Lily got in her car and started it before I shut the door and set the alarm.

I had been worried how I was going to sleep with Jasper gone, but after all the wine I drank I was exhausted. I climbed into bed and tossed and turned waiting for Lily's text. Finally, I gave up and grabbed the shirt that Jasper had worn yesterday and got back into bed. I pulled it close to my face and inhaled, sweat mixed with his deodorant filled my nose and calmed me. It was scary how in such a short amount of time I had become dependent on his smell. Lily texted me she was home, and I let sleep take me.

I wished Jasper was here.

Jasper

"Em, baby scoot over."

Emily blinked her eyes a few times before focusing on me.

"Huh? What time is it?" she asked.

"Almost four."

As much as I hated to disturb her, she was sprawled across the bed leaving no room for me to get in. I was so fucking tired. I debated spending the night in Montana, but after going to the cemetery, I couldn't wait to get home. I hadn't traveled all night to get back to her to sleep on the couch or Jason's bed. I needed to feel her.

She moved over, and one of my tees was in her hand. "Baby, why's my dirty shirt in the bed?"

"Because it smelled like you," she whispered in her sleep.

She rolled to her side, and I slipped in next to her wrapping my arms around her. Her breathing evened out, and I held her close. I could not lose this woman. And it had nothing to do with me needing to forget. That was my guilt talking. It had everything to do with the fact that she was the one. The one that I had to let go of my past for, the one who was my future.

"I love you, Emily."

***

EMILY

I had the most delicious dream last night that Jasper was in bed with me and whispered he loved me. It was so real that when I woke up the room even smelled like Jasper. I rolled over and checked the time. Jason and Connor wouldn't be back until dinner time so I had plenty of time to laze around before I had to run errands.

I did a double take and looked back at the night-stand. There was a shoebox and a red leather journal type book on top of it. I didn't remember those being there when I went to bed last night. I got up and went to the bedroom door slowly cracking it open. Jasper's voice came from the living room, and I tentatively tiptoed down the hall. Afraid I was walking to my execution. That's what it would've been if Jasper was home to tell me we were done.

Jasper caught sight of me, his eyes doing a full body scan much like he'd done the first day he met me. Finally he met my eyes and his lips flattened in a hard line. That could not be good. He talked for a moment longer, and I began to mentally prepare myself for the death blow he was about to give me. I was trying to come up with something to make him stay.

"Copy that. Listen, Emily's up. I have to talk to her, I'll call you back."

Jasper swiped the screen of his phone and put it on the table. He was shirtless and in a pair of low-slung athletic shorts. His upper body on full display, yet I couldn't bring myself to enjoy the view, I was too captivated by his gaze.

"Morning," he said.

"Good." I had to clear the lump in my throat. "Morning."

"About yesterday. Can we sit down and talk?" he asked. I didn't trust my voice to answer him. Instead, I walked to the couch and sat down. "I'll be right back, I have to get something."

He left me on the couch alone in my thoughts. The last few months played out in my mind, like a highlight reel. Every touch, every kiss, every sweet thing he had said to me. I remembered them all.

How he'd saved my son and helped Connor recover. Sent my mom on a trip. Even if today my heart was ripped out of my chest, I regretted none of it. I would go through the pain of losing him a hundred times, if it meant I had had him, even for a short while.

CHAPTER TWENTY-NINE

Jasper

This morning when I left a sleeping Emily in our bed, a few more things clicked into place. The first and most important thing was I was not going to let her leave me, no matter what. I would beg if I had to, but she and Jason were not walking out of my life. Emily was open and honest with me about everything; she trusted me, fully. I had not extended that to her, not entirely. I had never lied to her. She pretty much knew everything about me, with the exception of work. I trusted her, but not fully. Not the way she trusted me.

I had not believed she was strong enough to shoulder the pain I had felt. If I expected her to come to me with everything that hurt her or worried her, I had to do the same. And telling her about it wasn't the same as allowing her to go through it with me.

I grabbed the box and journal off the nightstand and walked back into the living room. I didn't sit on the couch next to her, instead on the floor at her feet.

Truth time.

"Thank you. Thank you for being strong when I was weak. Thank you for loving me enough to call me on my bullshit. You were right. I'm sorry I walked out of here yesterday. I promise you that will never happen again." I looked up at Emily, and she was crying. I couldn't stop now, I had to get this out. "You were right about everything. Yesterday, I went to Montana. I met with Liz's sister Reagan and then I went to the cemetery to talk to Liz and Alesha. Reagan gave me a journal that Liz had made for me. I read the first page. I was hoping that you would go through the box and read the rest of the journal with me." Emily was crying harder, her face in her hands. "Em, baby, you're gutting me. If you don't want to, I understand."

"No," she sobbed. "I want to. I want to be there for you. Thank you for trusting me."

"I'm sorry I made you feel that I didn't," I told her.

With shaky hands and the warmth of Emily's

touch on my shoulder, I reached for the box and braced myself. I heard a sharp intake of breath behind me when I opened the lid. There was the smallest pair of patent white baby girl shoes I'd ever seen nestled next to a folded cotton blanket that looked like it had smears of blood on it. I gently pulled the blanket out and unfolded it.

Alesha's hospital blanket.

I looked back in the box, and there were two hospital bands – one had Liz's name on it, the other was teeny tiny with Alesha's name handwritten in small letters. The last thing in the box was a baby onesie in pink camo with the words, *My daddy is my hero*, and a pair of dog tags printed around the neck.

Both Emily and I sat in silence looking at the items. This box was all I had of my daughter. I turned my head to kiss Emily's hand on my shoulder, her hand coming away wet. I hadn't realized I had started to cry, but once I noticed, I let go. I was safe here, safe with her. My body shook, and I sobbed, finally letting it out. Emily slipped to her knees on the floor next to me and enveloped me in her arms, Alesha's blanket between us. As sorry as I was for what I'd done, I couldn't hold onto the guilt anymore. I would never forget either of them, but I wouldn't let myself drown in my past either.

Emily pulled back and kissed my forehead, the same way I did her. "I love you, Jasper. All of you." She picked the book up and started to hand it to me.

"Will you do it? Read it to me?" I asked.

"Of course."

She sat down next to me and opened the book. She read the letter that Liz had written me first. When she was done, she looked at me with a broad smile full of love and strength.

"I can see why she was so special to you, she was a beautiful woman."

And Liz, much like Emily, was a genuinely good person with a heart of gold.

Emily held the book between us and started to read. Over the next few hours, we cried together and laughed at some of the entries. Liz had a way with words, she interjected humor where she could and added personal notes to me. All of her thoughts throughout her pregnancy were in the book. What was missing from her journal were spite and bitterness. She never said one bad thing about my absence, only that she knew I'd come around.

After we'd both had time to digest Liz's journal Emily turned to me. "You okay?"

"I am," I answered.

EMILY

Shocked would've been an understatement. I couldn't believe that Jasper went all the way to Montana and home again in one day. And when he asked me to read Liz's journal to him, he had effectively branded himself on my soul. His willingness to share something so personal with me without even knowing what was in the pages. Yet he trusted me to read them to him. He'd waited to come home to me before he opened the box. To share in something so heartbreaking with him cemented our bond. He might've started to construct the wall in which he wanted to hide behind, but quickly tore it down and let me in. Completely and totally.

And Liz? I was so sad not only for Jasper but the world that such a beautiful soul was taken so early. I felt like I knew her after reading her journal. She was funny, and witty, and so full of love and life. She wrote in one of her entries that she had dreamt of a Christmas dinner gathering. The dream occurred not long after she had found out that they were having a girl. She wrote that in her dream they were all laughing around a large table. Jasper was there with his wife and kids, and she was there with her husband and kids. They had come together as one large blended family around Alesha. She had been positive in their ability to parent together because she believed their friendship was so strong. I'd have to agree with her; they would've made it work. And I wished that dream could've come true, and I was the wife at that table. Another thing I loved: Liz never said mine, I, or me. Instead, she used we, us, together. Completely unselfish in her love for Alesha.

"Thank you for sharing that with me. I know it was difficult." I kissed his cheek.

"Em, I couldn't have done this without you."

I loved that. But, I was still a little nervous that even after all of this he still was holding onto the guilt instead of healing.

"How do you feel?" I asked.

I watched him closely, a gamut of emotions playing over his face. When he finally answered, my heart soared.

"Free." I didn't hide my relief from him, and he used his thumb to wipe my tears away. "I understand now. The pain will always be there, and that's okay. But I won't let the guilt stop me from having a future with you. I deserve to be happy. I deserve a future with you, and Emily, there is a future."

"And kids?" I hated to ask so soon, but I had to

know. It wasn't a deal breaker per se, but his reasons for not wanting them might be.

"Only after you marry me." He smiled.

"And if I said I wanted four more?"

"I'd say that you were trying to torture me. It would be my luck I'd give you four girls. Then Jason and I would be outnumbered, and I'd get grey hair. Not to mention I might have to get a second job at McDonald's to keep them all clothed. But, baby, if you want four or ten more, I don't care. As long as you are their mother, I say bring it."

"I love you, Jasper."

"I love you, Em. How about I feed my woman and we get to practicing on one of your four babies? Jason's already six, we don't want them too far apart."

"I thought you said you wanted to be married first?"

"That's coming and soon." He stood up and helped me up. "One more thing, you know how I asked you and Jason to live here?" I nodded. "Offer rescinded. I'm no longer asking, you and Jason live here, permanently."

"Okay," I whispered.

"Are you hungry?" he asked. I shook my head. "Fan-fucking-tasic, because I'm starving and we only have a few hours before Jason's home. I don't like to rush while I'm eating." He winked and picked me up giving me no choice but to wrap around him. He walked us to the bedroom and stopped by the bed. "I love you so damn much, Emily."

I didn't get a chance to respond before his lips were on mine, and all thoughts started to fade into the background. All except one.

He was free.

CHAPTER 30

Blake Porter

Fall 2004

"Holy hell, you see the arm on that boy?" my friend
Bee asked.

"Who cares about his arm? That boy is fine," my
other friend Lynn said.

"Will both y'all be quiet? Some of us *are trying* to
watch the game," I snapped.

There was a minute thirty left on the clock, and
Levi McCoy had just thrown a five-yard pass. We
were three yards away from winning this game.
Virginia might not be as well-known as Texas when
it came to football; however, we took our Friday
nights during football season real serious around

here. The crowd was on their feet and cheering; there was nothin' better than being in the stands watching a game under the lights. It was electrifying. Some Fridays I pulled out my new Motorola baby pink flip phone to record the crowd. I liked to listen to it when I was writing my article for the student paper. The normal spunk of the cheerleaders even seemed to be dialed up for tonight's game. I held my breath when the ball was snapped and Levi caught it, quickly looking for an open receiver. He faked right then took off left, dashing into the end zone when he saw a hole in the defensive line.

"That McCoy is somethin' else. You hear what Kasey said about him?" I guess Lynn hadn't answered fast enough because Bee went on. "They went out last Friday after the game, and *he* went down on *her*. How many juniors you know do that? All the boys I know want *you* to go down on *them*. Not the other way around."

I rolled my eyes at my two idiot friends. As smart as they were, they'd listen to any gossip that came around the bend. And our high school had plenty of it. Just last week I was seen making out with some freshman boy; that was the rumor anyway. It mustn't've been any good, because sure as shit, I couldn't even remember it.

"Blake, you comin' with us to the Tastee-Freez?" Lynn asked.

"Yeah. But I'll hike it home from there. I don't want to tag along to another house party in bum fuck Egypt only to have the troopers bust it ten minutes later."

"Whatever," Lynn mumbled.

We made our way out of the stadium to the student parking lot and piled into Lynn's pickup truck. The Tastee-Freez was already filling up by the time we got there, after stopping at the only convenience store that still accepted fake IDs. Lynn parked her truck next to some of the seniors and jumped out to go talk to them. I dumped my beer into a solo cup and followed Bee to the back of the truck. No sooner was the tailgate down and our asses planted on it, some baseball player that Bee had been tryin' to hook up with jumped up and pushed his way in between Bee and me.

"What the hell?" I muttered.

"Blake, Bee. How are you fine ladies this evenin'?" the guy crooned out.

"Hey Charlie," Bee gushed. Yes, she gushed, even though it was more in her body language than her tone of voice. She leaned in real close and pushed her impressive boobs into his arm.

I stopped listening to their conversation when a huge black F150 with a modified exhaust that made it so loud it was impossible to ignore, pulled into the parking lot. I continued to stare long after the truck's ignition was turned off and the noise had been silenced. I knew who'd be stepping out of the truck; the mystery was which cheerleader would be getting out with him.

Levi McCoy jumped out of the driver's side, freshly showered and dressed in a pair of jeans, black boots, and his normal button up flannel shirt. I would never admit this to anyone, but I'd had a crush on Levi since the first day of our freshman year when we had English class together. Over the years he had gotten bigger, better looking, and better on the football field. Now he looked like a full-grown man and had an ego to match. Even though most of the time he was an arrogant ass, I still couldn't stop crushing on him.

I watched as Levi made his rounds; all the popular kids congratulating him on tonight's win. Fist bumps and guy hugs complete with the back pounding were exchanged. A few girls ran up and kissed his cheek, vying for his attention. It really was interesting how the high school pecking order worked. The jocks were at the top of the pyramid, followed by the rich kids. Those two groups inter-changed. It was socially acceptable for a middle-class jock to associate with the wealthy kids that went to our school. But if you were a middle-class no one, such as myself, you'd never be accepted into the popular clique. We didn't dress the same, drive nice cars, and we certainly didn't have the same weekly allowances. Hell, my parents couldn't afford to give me an allowance. I had an afterschool job at the movie theatre.

Bored with people watching and finishing the one beer I could sneak and still go home without my parents noticing, I was about to tell Bee I was leaving when Levi walked up and stopped in front of us.

"Blake, right?" he asked.

I felt my cheeks heat hearing him say my name. I hadn't heard him call me by my name since the first day in English class and that was only because he needed to borrow a pen from me.

"That's me," I stupidly said.

'That's me'; those were my first words I spoke to the boy in almost three full years, not something witty or flirty like one of the cheerleaders would say.

"Thought so. I wanted to tell you I really enjoyed your article in last week's student paper."

I guess he would've liked it. I wrote a two-page

spread highlighting his football career at Dominion High School. Scouts were coming around now that he was a junior, trying to get him to early commit to one of their colleges. Rumor had it he was being recruited by five Division I schools, four of those five offering him a full ride if he'd commit. His superior arm gave him a huge advantage over all the other quarterbacks trying to garner the attention of the top schools.

"Glad you liked it. With all your wins it was easy to write. I hope I didn't leave anything out," I responded.

"Oh. The football write-up? That was cool, too. I think you made me sound better than I really am though." Say what? Was Levi McCoy humble? "It's a team effort. I know I get most of the credit, and it isn't fair. Did you know that James Pats has the most receiving yards in the state, and he is on course to beat the Wide Receiver Hall of Fame record?" Levi stopped, and I didn't know what to say. Was he upset I hadn't featured the rest of the team? My assignment was to highlight Levi. "Anyway, I was talking about the student mentoring and tutoring program you're starting. I'd like to volunteer. I can tutor math and science. I'm in AP Bio this semester and AP Calc."

And that was how my relationship with my long-time crush began; me sitting on Lynn's tailgate, an empty solo cup in my hand and a dumbfounded look on my face. He did help me set up the after-school tutoring, and he was an active volunteer. The more time we spent together, the closer we became and the more I got to know the real Levi McCoy, not the star quarterback everyone wanted a piece of. He told me he didn't want a football scholarship; he wanted to join the Army. His dream was to serve his country, not play football. I told him about wanting to be a journalist traveling the world, writing what I saw in faraway places.

The following two years were the best of my life. Even after his mom married Alister Bench, a media mogul, and his family became rich, my relationship with him didn't change. It remained strong despite Levi's wealth. Despite him changing schools. Despite leaving me all by myself. In fact, it allowed me to focus on writing for the student paper, where I became editor.

Life was great.

I was madly in love with the boy of my dreams. A month before graduation, Levi had driven us out to our special hiding spot. It was a secluded wooded area miles outside of town. We went there a lot when we wanted to be alone. It was the very spot I'd given him my virginity the year before. We parked and he swore me to secrecy, telling me he had enlisted in the Army. He had turned eighteen a few weeks before and no longer needed his mother's consent. I was proud that he was following his dreams but scared. After he'd explained everything, he laid me down on a blanket in the grass and made love to me. He told me I had nothing to worry about, that he loved me. After basic training, I would move to where he was stationed, and go to college there. We had a plan, a bright and happy future ahead of us.

Everything was perfect until Alister and Levi's mom found out he was leaving for the Army and not going to college to play football. My first mistake was trusting Alister Bench when he called and asked me to come by the house under the pretense he had a letter of recommendation for me to help me get into a summer writing clinic. I should've known something was wrong; the man hated me. He blamed me and my 'low-rent' family for putting 'classless ideas of military service' in Levi's head. I should've smelled the set-up long before I did. Alister quickly ushered me into his study when I arrived at the house. First, he offered me an internship at one of his newspapers if I would break up with Levi and tell him to scrap his military plans. When that didn't work, he offered me money, lots of it. He offered to pay for my college, pay off my parents' house, and buy me a car. The gifts he was willing to give were endless. The man was desperate for me to leave Levi. Through it all, my mind and heart never wavered. I allowed him to continue to bribe me. At eighteen-years-old I thought I could play with the big wig and win. Boy was I wrong. Just when I thought I had everything I needed to bring Alister Bench down the front door slammed shut.

That door ended up being a lot more than a rectangular piece of wood. It was my future, and it was lost to me. All the plans we had made, the love we had shared, all the hope I had of one day marrying Levi, crashed shut that afternoon. Every phone call, text message, every letter I wrote Levi while he was in basic training went unanswered. A few months after he should've graduated basic, his phone was disconnected.

He was gone.

My freshman year of college I made a promise to myself. One day, somehow, someway, I would destroy Alister Bench.

Blake Porter was one of the lucky ones. She'd met the man she was going to marry while she was in high school. She thought she was living a fairytale; the nerdy wannabe journalist dating the gorgeous star quarterback. One wrong move proved to irrevocably alter the course of their lives. Can Blake win back Levi and get back the future she always wanted?

Find out in Finally Free. Grab your copy now

Nightstalker

Protecting Olivia

Redeeming Violet

Recovering Ivy

Rescuing Erin

The Gold Team - Susan Stoker Universe

Brooks

Thaddeus

Kyle

Maximus

Declan

Blue Team - Susan Stoker Universe

Owen

Gabe

Myles

Kevin

Cooper

Garrett

The 707 Freedom Series

Free

Freeing Jasper

Finally Free

Freedom

The Next Generation (707 spinoff)

Saving Meadow

Chasing Honor

Finding Mercy

Claiming Tuesday

Adoring Delaney

Keeping Quinn

Taking Liberty

Triple Canopy

Damaged

Flawed

Imperfect

Tarnished

Tainted

Conquered

Shattered

Fractured

The Collective

Unbroken

Trust

Standalones

Romancing Rayne

Falling for the Delta Co-written with Susan Stoker

AUDIO

Are you an Audio Fan?

Check out Riley's titles in Audio on Audible and iTunes

Gemini Group

Narrated by: Joe Arden and Erin Mallon

Red Team

Narrated by: Jason Clarke and Carly Robins

Gold Team

Narrated by: Lee Samuels and Maxine Mitchell

The 707 Series

Narrated by: Troy Duran and C. J. Bloom

The Next Generation

Narrated by: Troy Duran and Devon Grace

Triple Canopy

Narrated by: McKenzie Cartwright and Connor Crais

More audio coming soon!

Riley Edwards is a USA Today and WSJ bestselling author, wife, and military mom. Riley was born and raised in Los Angeles but now resides on the east coast with her fantastic husband and children.

Riley writes heart-stopping romance with sexy alpha heroes and even stronger heroines. Riley's favorite genres to write are romantic suspense and military romance.

Don't forget to sign up for Riley's newsletter and never miss another release, sale, or exclusive bonus material.

Rebels Newsletter

Facebook Fan Group

www.rileyedwardsromance.com

facebook.com/Novelist.Riley.Edwards

instagram.com/rileyedwardsromance

bookbub.com/authors/riley-edwards

amazon.com/author/rileyedwards